Passions Fulfilled

Ardor Creek, Book 5

By

AYLA ASHER

Contents

Because it's never too late to find your soul mate, even if they've been right in front of you the whole time...

A Note from the Author

Well, dear readers, here we are again. If you've followed me on this Ardor Creek journey so far, you'll know I like to tackle subjects that are a bit off the beaten path. So far, we've had a widower, a recovered addict, and a woman who struggled with infertility. I really enjoy writing about real-life situations and seeing characters experience their happy ending after overcoming adversity.

Passions Fulfilled is no different. I fell in love with Justine and Gary in Desires Uncovered and knew halfway through that book they would need their own story. Of course, it's *me*, so I decided to tackle another real-life issue we don't see a lot in romance novels. Part of reading romance is the hot, steamy times, and as much as I love those, they're not always true to life. Gary experiences a trauma that affects his ability to perform in the bedroom. I thought it would be so sweet and fulfilling to see him and Justine learn how to navigate that often uncomfortable situation with openness and honesty and ultimately find happiness. This is a book about communication between partners and accepting the one you love no matter what. It was such a joy to write, and I hope you enjoy their HEA as much as I did.

Thank you for continuing the journey in Ardor Creek with me, and happy reading!

Prologue

♥

Gary Lincoln lifted his shoulder and spoke into the radio attached to his blue uniform.

"Officer down, need backup. Our 10-20 is the alley between Vance Appliances and the jewelry store on South Main Street. Do you copy?"

"10-4," a scratchy voice replied. "EMS is on the way. Multiple injuries?"

"The thief had a gun and shot Officer Craven in the leg." Crouching down, Gary examined his fellow officer as he wailed in pain. "I'll try to stop the bleeding until backup arrives."

"10-4. ETA, two minutes."

Pulling his shirt, he untucked it and ripped off a piece of fabric. Placing it over the officer's wound, he applied pressure.

"Stay with me, Chris," he said, noting the man's eyes begin to glaze over. "That bastard isn't going to get away with this."

Something shuffled to Gary's side, and he snapped his head. The thief stood frozen, panting as puffs of air appeared with each breath in the cold night.

"I have to go back and get the jewels," the thief said, glancing toward the alley that led to the front of the strip mall. "I have kids and haven't been able to get a job for two years." He began to inch forward, and Gary tensed.

"Stop! I'm not letting you anywhere near the jewelry store." Sliding his hand toward the gun attached to his belt, Gary tried like hell to keep the movement imperceptible. "Shooting a cop is a big offense, kid. You're in deep shit, and my backup will be here any minute. Your best bet is to run."

The man's eyes grew wide beneath the ski mask. Gary took the moment to memorize everything he could about the man's build in the dim light. He couldn't be more than twenty-five, and sadly, he'd go to jail for tonight's actions for a very long time. Of that, Gary was sure. He was a damn good cop, and he'd track every lead until they caught the bastard. Confident in his skills, he told the kid to run, deciding it was more important to keep pressure on Chris's wound.

"I...I can't," he said, lifting the gun, hand shaking. "I have to get the jewels. Let me pass, or I'll shoot you."

Grasping his gun, Gary slowly stood, frustrated he had to stop applying pressure to his bleeding friend's wound. "Don't make me shoot you," he said, showing the thief his palm.

"I'm sorry," he said, swiping his nose. "I never meant for this to happen."

The next moments happened in a flash—a nightmare Gary would never forget. He drew his gun as the thief discharged his weapon. Gary's gun fired the second he felt the bullet enter his upper thigh. Pain exploded in every cell of his body as the burglar grunted and fell to the ground. Clutching his thigh, Gary toppled over, feeling the blood gush over his leg.

"Gary!" Chris called, still writhing in pain. "You hit, man?"

"Yeah," Gary said, his voice hollow to his ears as he strove to retain consciousness. "Think he hit an artery. I'm bleeding out."

Ambulances sounded in the distance as Gary used the last of his strength to lift his head and look at the thief. He was still upon the cold ground and most likely dead. Gary had meant to shoot him in the shoulder, but it was possible he shot him in the heart. Sadly, he realized he might not live long enough to find out. Unable to support the weight of his head, it fell to the ground, and he closed his eyes.

An infinity later, sounds rustled above, and Gary felt himself being transported—to heaven, hell, or the hospital, he had no damn idea. And then, all he heard was the beeping of a monitor that slowly evolved into a buzzing in his brain...which eventually turned into the deepest silence Gary had ever experienced.

Chapter 1

Eight years later...

Gary Lincoln sat in his favorite recliner, absently massaging his thigh as he watched the Steelers play. They were losing, but he had faith they'd come back in the fourth quarter. Sipping his beer, he relaxed in his chair, happy to have the day off. He'd been picking up a lot of overtime lately since he'd finally decided he was ready to buy a house. His buddy Peter had helped him make a financial plan, and he figured he would be ready to start looking in a year. This had only been exacerbated by the fact his ex-wife was remarrying and he would finally be free from alimony payments.

"Speak of the devil," he murmured as his phone buzzed on the small side table. Lifting it to his ear, he answered. "Hey, Nicole."

"Hey," she said, her voice even and free of the anger they'd both held after their divorce. They were on much better terms in recent years, and Gary was thankful for their progression. "I'm calling about the alimony. I'm going to be closing my account so I can open a joint account with Patrick. Would you mind just sending me the last payment by paper check?"

"Sure. Should I send it to your apartment or Patrick's house?"

"You can send it to Patrick's. I'll be moving in with him next week before the wedding in late October. I'll text you the address. Everything's all set with the courts, and my attorney has wrapped everything up. One last check and we'll finally be free of each other."

He traced his finger over his worn jeans as he nodded. "Yep. I hope he makes you happy, Nicole."

A soft sigh echoed over the phone before silence stretched between them. Eventually, she spoke. "I'm sorry everything ended the way it did. I look back now and realize I made so many mistakes. I just didn't know how to handle things when you got shot and...well, afterward."

"We grew apart. It happens. Everyone told us we were too young to get married."

She breathed a laugh, and he could almost see her grin on the other side of the phone. "We should've listened to them. Our entire relationship was based on our teenage hormones. Once those dwindled, I just don't think we had anything in common."

The statement was imminently true since they were as different as two people could be. Gary was stoic—which was perfect for his job as a cop—and he'd always been a bit shy. He didn't enjoy hanging out in loud bars where people spoke at the top of their lungs and got tipsy. Hell, he policed those same bars and ensured people remained safe on their way home after the establishments closed. Ride share apps were a godsend, and drunk driving had been on a steady decline for the past few years.

Nicole, on the other hand, would hang out until the sun came up. She had limitless energy and was always finding some sort of mischief to get into. It had been extremely attractive to him when she moved to Ardor Creek their senior year. Several of his friends had set their sights on her, but for some reason, she'd been drawn to him. They started dating, lost their virginities to each other, and were married by the tender age of twenty. Looking back now, he understood they'd moved too quickly. Sex between them had been great, but they soon learned that was their one uniting factor.

Gary entered the police academy soon after their marriage and threw himself into his role as a patrol officer as soon as he was hired at the Ardor Creek Police Department. His dad had been Chief Deputy in the Lackawanna County Sheriff's Office, instilling Gary's desire to follow in his footsteps. He enjoyed patrol work and eventually became Patrol Captain, which meant he supervised all the other patrol officers.

On his rise to Patrol Captain, he'd worked tirelessly and took full responsibility for not giving enough attention to his marriage. Nicole worked part-time as a nail tech in a local salon and grew increasingly frustrated at his work schedule. Eventually, she began to go out alone, seeking companionship from her girlfriends. The one connection that remained was their sexual connection, which had always been explosive. Then, Gary got shot, and it all went to shit.

"Gary?" she asked, dragging him from his thoughts. "Did I lose you?"

"I'm here," he said, sipping his beer. "My mind wandered. Sorry."

"Anyway, not to make this more awkward, but I'll apologize one last time for cheating. I'm not sure when we'll have the chance to talk again, and it's important I say it before we move on for good."

Chances were, they might never speak or see each other again. Her fiancé lived in Virginia Beach, and she had no ties to Ardor Creek since her parents had passed away and her sister lived in California. According to the gossip mill, which was rampant in their small town, Nicole had met Patrick online a year ago. They'd had an instant connection, and he'd visited her a few times in Ardor Creek before he began flying her down to Virginia. They'd fallen in love and were now getting married. Gary was genuinely happy for her and truly wished her well. The last few years of their marriage had been miserable, and it would be nice for her to experience a loving, healthy relationship with her new husband.

"I got over it years ago, Nicole," he said, sighing. "Hell, part of me doesn't blame you."

"You're being unfair to yourself, Gary," she said, her tone compassionate. "And you should probably hate me, but I'm happy you don't. It's nice to be able to be cordial with you after everything."

"Life's too short to waste it being angry," he said, repeating the words his dad had often said. Gary had always looked up to his dad, who was inherently kind and well-respected, and he strove to be half the man he was. "I just don't have the energy anymore."

"Said like a man who just turned forty-three," she teased.

"Good lord, don't remind me, woman."

"Hey, I'll be forty-three in a month, and I've never felt better. Falling in love again has done wonders for my skin. Everyone says I'm glowing. Maybe you should fall in love again too. Of course, that would mean you'd have to do something besides work and occasionally hang with your buddies."

An image of Justine Lancaster's face flitted through his brain before he immediately shut it down. Regardless of Nicole's gentle insistence, he was nowhere ready to enter into any sort of relationship again. The last one had failed miserably, and he wasn't really a fan of repeating terrible mistakes.

"I'm fine being solo. It allows me to focus on what I really love, which is helping the people of Ardor Creek."

"Okay, Officer Lincoln," she said, amusement in her tone. "But let me just say something—"

"Nicole—"

"No, I need to say this, Gary. I was...harsh with you," she said, pausing to find the right word. "At the time, it stemmed from my frustration, and I wish I could take back half the things I said. But I need you to believe me when I tell you that there's someone out there who will love you exactly the way you are. You're a good man, and I firmly believe that."

"I'm getting love advice from my ex-wife," he muttered, rubbing his eyes. "Were you *trying* to make this conversation as awkward as possible?"

Her soft chuckle drifted over the phone. "Not really, but we were the poster children for awkward at the end of our marriage, weren't we?"

"Yeah," he said, pulling at a stray thread on his jeans.

"Anyway, remember what I said. I hope you find happiness too. Thank you for not hating me. It says a lot about you, Gary."

"Be well, Nicole. Text me Patrick's address and I'll get the check out to you this week. Just have your lawyer reach out to mine so we can close this chapter."

"Will do. Bye."

Clicking off the phone, he tossed it on the table and heaved a labored breath. Although he'd forgiven Nicole, speaking to her dredged up all the old pain and heartache. It now lurked just beneath the surface, thick and murky, and he stood, feeling the need to take a walk. It was a warm day for late September, and he could walk a mile or so before the fourth quarter of the game kicked into high gear.

And he could also walk by Justine's house, just to make sure she and Avery were safe inside.

Resolved that both the walk and checking on his girls would make him feel better, he tugged on his light jacket and sneakers. Of course, they weren't *his* girls, although he realized he inwardly referred to them as that more and more. Telling himself to get his head out of the clouds, he headed outside into the sunny afternoon. The walk would also stretch his thigh muscles, which would hopefully reduce the slight throbbing he'd felt earlier.

He walked several blocks, eventually entering Justine's cul-de-sac. Her car wasn't in the driveway, so they must be out. Perhaps at her parents' or her brother, Mark's. Or maybe she'd finally met someone. It had been over a year since her divorce from her shithead ex-husband, and a woman as pretty and talented as Justine wouldn't be single for long. Gary knew this and had already steeled his heart for the moment he saw her around Ardor Creek with a new boyfriend. As long as she was happy, he would do his best to be happy for her too.

After all, when you loved someone as deeply as he loved Justine Lancaster, that person's happiness was of the utmost importance.

Even if Gary knew it would be with someone else.

Shaking his head to clear the dreary thoughts, he continued on his walk and returned home to watch the end of the fourth quarter. The Steelers did indeed make a comeback and ended up beating the Bills by ten points. Lifting his beer, he gave a salute, acknowledging the bright spots of the day. His team had won, and he was about to write his last alimony check. All in all, life was pretty damn good.

Chapter 2

Justine Lancaster secured the last of her mother's amazing lasagna leftovers in the storage container, excited she wouldn't have to cook for at least two days. She and Avery could definitely survive on lasagna and brownies, which they could make together tomorrow after she got home from school. It wasn't really a diet of champions, but Justine didn't give a damn. They could eat healthily later in the week once she'd had time to go to the market.

"Avery?" she called, wondering where her daughter had run off to. "It's time to head home so we can get a good night's sleep before school tomorrow."

Her daughter zoomed into the kitchen, Mark chasing close behind as she giggled. He caught her, lifting her high in the air and giving her a raspberry as she wriggled in his arms. Avery squealed in delight before he set her on the ground and she grinned up at him.

"Again!" she cried.

"Uh, that's enough, Uncle Mark," Justine said, walking over and encircling his arm to prevent him from lifting her. "We're supposed to be winding down for bed. Some of us have big things to accomplish in second grade tomorrow."

Mark and Avery formed twin pouts, making them look adorable, and Justine laughed. "Okay, you two are ganging up on me. So not fair." Handing the container to Avery, she said, "Go put this in the car while I give one last hug to Teresa and Rose, please."

Grasping the container, Avery zipped out of the kitchen, causing Justine to expel a breath.

"Man, she has so much energy," she said, rubbing her forehead. "Did we have that much energy?"

Their mother chose that moment to breeze into the kitchen. "Mark was always very well-behaved, but you certainly had a rebellious streak, Justine. I think Avery might be giving you a taste of your own medicine."

"Thanks for the reminder you had *one* perfect child," Justine muttered, rolling her eyes. "Glad you were able to suffer through raising me."

"Oh, stop it right now, dear," Brenda said, wiping the counter. "You both are wonderful, and I'm so lucky to have you. And now, we have Avery and Rose..." Her eyes watered as she held her fist to her lips. "Well, we're all so lucky."

"Okay, Mom, let's ditch the waterworks," Justine said, striding over to rub her shoulder. "We're all finally happy. There's no reason to cry." Glancing at Mark, she playfully rolled her eyes.

Her brother smirked before sliding onto one of the stools that lined the kitchen island. "We *are* really lucky," he said. "And I'm happy you two are on good terms. Let's not ruin it."

Justine smiled at her mom before giving her a quick hug, acknowledging the strides they'd made in their relationship. Brenda hadn't always approved of her decision to follow her passion and become an artist, which had been a point of contention between them. Now that Justine had built a solid career around her art, Brenda had finally come around. Her mother also hadn't approved of her marriage to Dean Rodgers, which had fueled several furious arguments between them. Now that she was divorced from the bastard, Justine was self-aware enough to admit Brenda had been right.

Justine met Dean during those weird transition years after high school where you were no longer a student but didn't know what the heck you wanted to do with your life. She'd always wanted to pursue an artistic path and was a gifted sculptor, drawer, and painter. She didn't acknowledge those things about herself with any sort of arrogance—they just happened to be the talents she was born with. Mark, on the other hand, was pretty much a genius, which led to him becoming a successful attorney and, eventually, the District Attorney of Lackawanna County. He'd gotten the brains, and she'd gotten the creative genes. Her dad was excellent at sketching, although he only did it for fun, but Justine figured he'd passed the artistic genes down to her.

Dean had seemed so exciting to her when they first met. He was a bit of a rebel who drank too much and smoked weed he purchased from mysterious people who piqued Justine's curiosity. Ardor Creek had always seemed quite boring to her, and Dean had swept her off her feet with his good looks and charm. He'd also treated her like shit, even in the early days, but for some reason, that had made Justine want him even more. He'd look at her, eyes glazed and joint in hand, and tell her she was so lucky to be with him. He was three years older and had seemed so mature while she wondered how to even begin selling the art she loved to create.

She moved in with him two months after they started dating, which incensed her mother, and very quickly thereafter, Dean began to threaten to kick her out.

"You know, I could have anyone, Justine," he would say while puffing on a cigarette or joint, which always made their apartment smell terrible. "Don't get too comfortable here because I might get tired of you."

She would always laugh the statements off as a joke, making the excuse he had a dry sense of humor that most just didn't get. It was the beginning of many times in her life when Justine would make excuses for Dean's terrible behavior.

They fell into a pattern, Justine becoming more and more fearful he would leave her. If that happened, she would have to admit she'd been wrong and return to her parents' house with her tail between her legs. Justine vowed it would never happen. So, she fought. Fought for their relationship, and, eventually, began to fight more with Dean. In those early years, she saw flashes of anger, and he even lifted his hand to her on occasion, but he never struck her.

Eventually, she became pregnant with Avery, and for one small moment in time, they were truly happy. Dean seemed excited by the news and had just received a promotion at his job as a factory supervisor at one of the nearby packing plants. They bought their home in a nice cul-de-sac in Ardor Creek, and Justine felt they'd finally turned the page.

The first few months after Avery was born, everything was quite normal. And then, Dean came home drunk and their life began the downward spiral that ultimately led to their divorce. She'd just put Avery to bed and was watching TV when he barreled into the living room and tried to kiss her. He wreaked of booze and cigarettes, and she was so disgusted she pushed him away. Rage had filled his light blue eyes before he crashed the back of his hand into her cheek. Shocked and terrified, she'd sat frozen on the couch as he crouched before her, breaking into tears and giving a heartfelt apology. He promised he would never hurt her again and begged her forgiveness, which she reluctantly gave.

Looking back, Justine understood that first time was the gateway to larger transgressions. It had shown Dean she would forgive him even if he hurt her. Armed with that knowledge, he made her life a living hell. She worked hard to be the wife he wanted, always having dinner on the table and keeping the house clean so he wouldn't get angry when he got home. Her art had taken a back seat to being a wife and mother, and she barely pursued it. When she began to hear rumors he was cheating, Justine dismissed them and worked harder, believing if she put the work in at home, he'd have no reason to look anywhere else. Because no matter what, after all the violence and discord, Justine still loved him.

During those years, Avery was her one bright spot of happiness. Her daughter was the most important thing in the world, and Dean was a passable father, even if he was a bit absent. Justine did her best to fill the void, leading to an extremely close mother-daughter bond between them. Although Justine made excuses when Dean was rough with her, she knew in her heart he would never hit Avery.

Until he did. That fateful night over two years ago had changed everything, and Justine still remembered it as if it were yesterday. She and Dean were arguing in the kitchen after Avery headed to her bedroom to play on her tablet before bed. Justine couldn't even remember what the argument had been about, although it was likely Dean's increasing absence at home...or his proclivity to being seen in cars with other women after an evening at the pub. Either way, Justine was furious and said something nasty, and he backhanded her. For some reason, the urge to fight back had swelled deep within, and she charged him. He grasped onto her neck and squeezed as stars burst behind her eyelids. At that moment, she realized he might actually kill her.

Unbeknownst to her, Avery had been hiding behind the door-frame watching them, and she ran toward them, tugging Dean away by his free arm. He released Justine, but in his wrath, he pivoted toward Avery and crashed his hand against her face so hard Justine felt it in her bones. Terrified for her little girl, Justine had grabbed the knife on the counter and swiped, cutting Dean in several places on his arms. He lunged for her, lost his balance, and hit his head on the corner of the kitchen island on the way down. As he bled out on the white tile floor, Justine called Mark, not knowing what the hell do to, and thus began her final descent into the end of her marriage to Dean.

"Did we lose you, Jus?" Mark asked, waving his hand and jerking her from the memories.

"Uh, no," she said, shaking her head. "Just got lost thinking about the time I went to jail for attempted murder of my ex-husband. Fun memories all around."

"Thank goodness he's out of our lives," Brenda said with a harumph. "Now, you can move on and find someone better. I still say you should cuddle up to that nice policeman who always looks out for you two. Mark tells me he drives by your house during his patrol shifts to check on you. It's just so sweet."

"Gary has his own life, Mom," she said, rolling her eyes. "Unless he's interested in train wreck divorcees whom he booked for mur-der with a kid and a crap-ton of baggage. On second thoughts, I'm definitely a catch. Can't understand why he hasn't swept me off my feet."

"You never know," Mark said, arching a brow. "Gary's a good guy."

Narrowing her eyes, Justine noticed her brother's shit-eating grin. "Do you know something I don't know? If you're holding out on me, you're toast."

"I know nothing," he said, showing her his palms. "Except I might have heard Nicole is remarrying and moving to Virginia Beach. His marriage is as officially over as yours. That's all I'm saying."

"They got divorced years ago," Justine said, shrugging. "It's been over for a while."

"Kind of like your marriage," Mark said, arching a brow.

"Um, okay, as much as I loooooove these cryptic conversations with you," she said sardonically, crossing her arms, "I have a kid I need to get ready for school tomorrow. Where's my little Rosie? I need to hug her before I go."

Standing, Mark trailed to her side and slid his arm over her shoulders before leading her to the living room. "You know I've forbidden you to call her Rosie, right?"

"And that's exactly why I do it," she said, beaming up at him as she batted her eyelashes.

"You're a pain in my ass," he muttered.

"But you love me anyway." Disengaging from him, she walked over to the couch, where Teresa was feeding their daughter a bottle. "There's my little Rosie. Aunt Jus needs to hug you before I go."

Teresa drew back the bottle and Justine lifted the precious little girl in her arms, kissing her swath of dark hair. Mark and Teresa had adopted Rose in a closed adoption earlier that year, and Justine thought her the cutest baby she'd ever seen—since Avery, of course.

"You're getting so big!" Justine said, using her "baby talk" voice as she lifted Rose in the air before lowering her to kiss her cheek. "Who's your favorite aunt in the world? Aunt Justine!" she said, cradling Rose in the crook of her arm and pointing at herself.

"Don't tell my brother's wife," Teresa teased when Mark sat beside her, sliding his arm around her shoulders. "She'll be devastated."

"It will be our little secret, won't it, Rosie?"

"Justine—" Mark warned.

"Okay, okay," she said, handing Rose back to Teresa. "I'm just doing it to annoy you now. You two look so cute holding her. A sweet little family. I'm so happy for you guys." Feeling her eyes well, she breathed a laugh. "Damn, now I'm crying like Mom. Good grief."

"You heading out, honey?" Joseph asked, trailing over to hug her.

"Sure am. See you next weekend, Dad."

Avery ran back inside, her stuffed rabbit tucked close to her side. "The car's loaded, Mom. Come on." She gave a dramatic eye roll. "I need to brush my teeth so I can get some sleep before school."

Looking at Mark and Teresa, Justine asked, "Does she get that dramatic streak from me?"

"Yes," they both said in unison, their voices deadpan.

"Wow, tough room. Okay, let's go, Sleeping Beauty. See you guys later."

They gave one last round of hugs before she loaded into the car, Avery strapped into the back seat with her tablet. The drive from her parents' house was short, and when they arrived home, Avery hurried inside to get ready for bed. Patting herself on the back for being an amazing parent whose kid *wanted* to go to bed, Justine decided she deserved a glass of wine once Avery was asleep.

Once her pajamas were on, Avery climbed into bed and Justine read her a story, savoring the fact she still let her perform the deed. Soon, her baby would be too old to want her mother to read to her, and that day would most likely break Justine's heart. After all, now that her marriage was long gone and Dean would never be in their lives again—thanks to the ironclad restraining order Mark had helped her file—Justine was invariably alone. Avery was her one companion, and she was growing up so fast Justine wished she could stop time. Realizing every mother probably felt this way, she stacked the book on the shelf and tucked Avery into bed.

"Good night, sweet princess," she said, kissing her forehead.

"Good night, sweet prince," Avery said, snickering at the silly phrases they always uttered before bedtime.

Pausing at the doorframe, Justine's hand rested above the light switch. "Want to make brownies tomorrow to have for dessert after we eat the lasagna leftovers?"

Avery's eyes widened, and she nodded. "Can we take some to Gary like we did last time? He said he ate them all in one helping. He must really like them."

Grinning, she nodded. "Sure thing, jelly bean. He's a really nice man, isn't he?"

Avery furiously shook her head and snuggled into the covers. "Night, Mom."

"Night, baby." Flicking off the light, she headed downstairs.

After pouring a glass of wine, Justine sat at the kitchen island, surrounded by silence as she contemplated. Glancing at the island corner, she noted it had long been cleaned, so all traces of Dean's blood were gone. Since the night was so horrific, Brenda had urged Justine to move and had even offered to let them live with her. Although their relationship had improved, Justine knew living with her mother again would drive her insane.

During the finalization of her divorce, Justine had agreed to take full ownership of the house in exchange for Dean not getting visitation rights and not having to pay alimony. It had seemed the best outcome for her since she wanted nothing to do with the bastard ever again. She'd also petitioned the court to change her and Avery's last name, and they'd recently become Lancasters again. Justine was finally free.

But there was a loneliness in being free, and Justine wondered if it would ever go away. She cherished Avery to her core, but she missed being held by someone who loved her—or who *claimed* to love her at least. Dean was her only lover, and she had enjoyed sex until he began hitting her. After that...well, it had been hard to enjoy opening her body to someone who was so violent. He usually initiated sex during his apology phase—those times after he hurt her where he swore it would never happen again. It made the sex between them uncomfortable—for her at least—and she wondered what it would feel like to make love with someone who was tender and loving. Dean had made an effort to please her during the early years, but eventually, he became a selfish lover, and she usually ticked off the seconds in her head until it was over.

"You need to try again, Jus," she murmured to herself, sipping her wine. But with whom? She wasn't joking about being the absolute worst catch in Ardor Creek. The knife wounds she'd inflicted on Dean had landed her in jail for attempted murder. Mark had eventually secured her acquittal and helped extricate Dean from their lives, but she was still damaged goods. What the hell would she put on her dating profile? *Attempted murderess with cute kid wants to find out if sex can be good when someone doesn't backhand you first.*

Uh, yeah, probably not a good look.

Staring at the island corner, she remembered how helpful Gary had been the night she got arrested. They'd become friends over the years, and she liked him immensely. He lived close by, and she would always catch him making rounds in his patrol car—not that there was a ton of crime in Ardor Creek. But every town had its criminals, and Gary was a fixture on the police force.

Justine liked to take walks since they helped clear her head and fuel her creativity. More often than not, Gary would cruise by in his patrol car, giving a wave and making her feel extremely safe. He'd also been the one who responded to the handful of 911 calls she made over the years when Dean hit her. On several occasions, Justine swore she'd had enough and called the cops, threatening Dean she would finally out him as an abuser. But every time, like clockwork, he would talk her off the ledge, apologize profusely, and tell her he loved her. And every time, she let the bastard get away with it.

Justine remembered one such night a few years ago when Gary had shown up at her door.

"Hi, Jus," he'd said, craning his neck to look into the foyer. "Dispatch says you called 911. Can I come in?"

"No," she said, rapidly shaking her head. "It's fine. False alarm. Everything's totally fine, and I'm sorry we bothered you guys."

His deep brown eyes had stared into her, filled with equal parts compassion, anger, and disbelief. That particular night, he'd reached behind her, clutching the doorknob and pulling the front door closed, forcing her onto the front porch.

"He can't hear you with the door closed, Justine," he said, his voice low and steady. "I can drive you and Avery to the station and help you file a restraining order. I promise I'll help keep you both safe."

Swallowing thickly, she forced a smile. "We're fine, Gary." Clutching his hand, she squeezed. "I'm sorry I caused such a mess. Please let the dispatcher know it was a false alarm."

His eyes roved over her face as he reached in his pocket. Pulling out a pack of toothpicks, he clenched one in his teeth before placing the pack back in his pocket. Lazily chewing, he regarded her.

"Um, so, yeah. This is nice and all, but seriously, we're fine. You can go now."

Slowly, he backed down the porch stairs and stared up at her. He maneuvered the toothpick between his lips as he considered. Finally, he withdrew it and held it between his fingers as he spoke. "I'll be parked out here for a few hours," he said, gesturing to his patrol car parked along the sidewalk. "You can just walk outside if you need me."

"Oh, that's not necessary—"

"It's not up for discussion, Jus." With a tip of his head, he turned to walk toward the car. "You stay safe."

"Thank you, Gary," she called, wishing she had the strength to actually file the restraining order. But Justine was determined to make the marriage work no matter what. God, she'd been so damn stupid.

"Teresa would tell you to cut the negative inner dialogue," she murmured, swirling her wine as she recalled the memories. Funnily enough, the thing she remembered most about that night was Gary rolling the toothpick on his tongue. Something about the way he'd maneuvered it between his firm lips and straight white teeth had spurred a weird tingling in her gut. Was it desire? Hell, she had no idea since she'd only ever felt desire for one man and was pretty sure it was all sorts of fucked up.

Closing her eyes, she imagined Gary kissing her with those broad lips then trailing them down to her breasts. Would he close those perfect teeth over her nipple and tug? Or maybe work her nipple on his tongue in the smooth way he'd worked the toothpick. Feeling flushed, Justine rubbed the back of her neck before chugging the rest of her wine.

Standing, she located the brownie batter in the cabinet. To-morrow, she and Avery would make a batch and take some to Gary. They'd done so two months ago, and he'd smiled as if they'd brought him a plate of gold. He truly did seem to enjoy it when they stopped by and had been nothing but gracious to her. Hell, he'd been more than gracious.

When she was arrested, Gary had personally overseen her book-ing and accompanied her in the back of the police cruiser to county jail. He'd ensured Mark would get temporary custody of Avery while she was incarcerated and had helped expedite the restraining orders when she finally filed them upon her release. Now, he regularly patrolled their block to confirm their safety, although Justine didn't fear Dean returning. He'd met some hot young thing in Battle Falls—according to the Ardor Creek gossip mill—and was supposedly on the fast-track to marriage. Shiver-ing, Justine rubbed her upper arms, hoping like hell he wouldn't be violent with his new flame, although people like Dean rarely changed in her experience.

Sighing, she washed the wineglass and set it in the rack before flipping off the light and heading to bed. Yes, tomorrow they'd visit Gary and bring him some brownies for being such a nice guy. Basically, for being the antithesis of Dean. And Justine would have another look at those luscious lips of his—strictly for research purposes, of course. Because if she knew one thing, the chances that the guy who'd processed her arrest and moved mountains to clean up her messes wanted anything to do with her romantically were about zero to never-gonna-fucking-happen. And Justine was practical enough not to waste time on things that weren't meant to be.

Which made it all the more interesting when she finally fell asleep that night and had a vivid sex dream about none other than Gary Lincoln in his police uniform, using his handcuffs in very naughty but exceedingly pleasurable ways.

Chapter 3

Gary ended his shift around six o'clock. It was an hour later than he expected, but Edna Schultz had called 911 mad as a hornet that her neighbor hadn't cleaned up his dog's excrement on her lawn. Gary had headed over and calmed the elderly woman down before ensuring her neighbor, a young kid who seemed scared to death of her, picked up the waste. Afterward, he'd headed inside for a slice of Edna's magnificent apple pie, chalking up the late call as a win-win while his tastebuds sang.

Once home, he parked his patrol car in the driveway of his two-bedroom rented home and unfolded from the car. He was six feet, two inches tall and scrunching his body into a patrol car five days a week didn't do him any favors. Feeling his thigh throb, he walked inside, noticing his small limp, and decided he'd apply the heat pad once he was settled in his recliner with a beer.

After closing the front door behind him, he removed his gun, ensuring the safety was on, and placed it in the drawer. Then, he placed his duty belt on the front table and began to unbutton his shirt. A knock sounded at the door, and he swiveled his head, wondering who it could be. Drawing it open, he found a beaming Justine and Avery Lancaster on the other side.

"Hi, Gary!" Avery said, adorable as she held Justine's hand. "Mom and I made brownies, and we wanted you to have some."

"Really?" he asked, unable to contain his grin. "You all know I love your brownies."

"I'm sorry for showing up unannounced," Justine said, her eyes darting to the exposed skin of his chest where he'd released a few buttons. "I figured it would be a nice surprise. Here you go." She thrust a plastic container toward him.

"Thanks," he said, pulling off the top and inhaling the aroma. "Yum, these smell so good. Want to come in and have one with me?"

"I...uh...oh, we don't want to impose. You look like you just got home."

"I did," he said, lifting a shoulder, "which means I'm starving. Why don't you all come into the kitchen and I'll set you up with some milk before I head up to change out of this uniform?" Stepping back, he jerked his head. "Come on."

"Yay!" Avery said, bounding inside and down the hallway.

"Thanks," Justine said, grinning as she stepped inside. "I should've realized you'd just be getting home. We had an early dinner and made brownies, and I wanted to stop by before bedtime."

He kicked off his shoes and urged her to follow him down the hallway. They'd been to his home before, so they knew the layout, and Avery was already sitting on one of the stools at his center island. "They're definitely better if you dip them in milk," she said, giving him a gap-toothed grin. "And we need to heat them in the microwave."

"Yes, ma'am," Gary said with a salute. Opening the cabinet, he selected a plate and set it on the island. "Take out three brownies and put them on here. The microwave's right up there," he said, pointing to it. Opening the fridge, he pulled out the milk and then located three glasses before setting them on the island. "Let me go change and I'll be right back."

Bounding up the stairs, Gary realized he'd forgotten all about his bum leg. Hell, who could think about pain when the woman of your dreams and her adorable daughter were waiting for you in your kitchen? Removing his uniform, he dressed in jeans and a t-shirt before heading back downstairs in bare feet. Entering the kitchen, he noticed Avery's wide-mouthed expression as Justine knelt on the floor wiping up milk.

"We spilled it," Avery said in a hushed tone as he approached.

"I'm not even going to *try* to make a joke about spilled milk," Justine said, her arm working in furious movements on the floor.

The luscious globes of her ass thrust high in the air in her tight jeans, and Gary felt a stirring inside his boxer briefs. Interesting, since things didn't really work all that well in that region after he'd been shot.

"It's okay," he said, kneeling and taking the cloth from Justine. He wiped up the last few drops before extending his hand, helping her as they both rose. "See? All gone."

"Thank goodness you had a full carton. I'll buy you another one to replace this one since we only have enough left for one round." Lifting the milk, she poured it into the three cups and shook the container. "Yep, doneski."

"You don't have to buy me more milk, Justine," he said, chuckling as he took the carton and threw it in the recycling bin. "Are the brownies in the microwave?"

"Yes, but they're probably cold now," Avery said, her lips forming a pout.

"Well, let's nuke 'em again." Picking her up, he balanced her on his hip and showed her how to use the microwave. "Hit the 'one' and then the 'zero,'" he directed, and her tiny fingers pushed the buttons. "Now, hit 'cook.'"

She depressed the button and gave him a cheeky grin.

"Good job. That should do it."

The microwave dinged, and Gary pulled out the brownies, setting them on the island before sliding onto a stool. Avery climbed on the stool beside him, and Justine sat across from them. "Dig in," he said, grabbing a brownie before dipping it in the milk. Avery did the same and took a huge bite, chewing before grinning at him with brownie-stained teeth.

"Not your best look, kid," he teased, taking a bite of brownie, "but you're still pretty darn cute."

"Thank you," she said, leaning into him. "Mom and I like sharing brownies with you."

"Well, I like it when you make brownies. Thank you for sharing."

Avery sidled against his arm, and Justine gave him a knowing grin. "She's enamored with you, you know?"

"What's enamored?"

"It means you really like him. And please stop squirming, because the stool is tall, and I don't want you to fall."

Avery scowled before settling on the stool.

"How was your day? Don't you have another showcase coming up soon?"

"Yes," Justine said, taking a sip of milk. "It's at Kristoff's gallery on Main Street. I have no idea why a fancy gallery owner from New York City decided to set up a gallery in Ardor Creek, but it's been a godsend. He loves my work and features it every time he does a show. And he's also displayed me in his gallery on Bleeker Street in the city, which is the primary source of my income. Who knew all those rich city dwellers would like paintings and sculptures from little ol' Justine Lancaster from Ardor Creek?"

"I knew," Gary said, swallowing a bite of brownie. "You're really talented, Jus."

"I have a feeling you're not a fan of my weird art, but you've shown up to every gallery show I've done so far. It's so nice, Gary, but you don't have to come if you're busy. I appreciate the support."

"It's easy for me to stop by when I'm on patrol," he said, shrugging. "And when I'm not, it gives me something to do. Besides the occasional barbeque with the gang and karaoke night at the pub, there's not a ton to do in Ardor Creek."

"Well, I'm glad I'm an alternative to severe boredom," she teased, biting her lip.

"No way—"

"Kidding," she said, sliding her hand over his. "You'll never know how much I appreciate your support. If I'm not careful, I'm going to begin to rely on you being there for every showcase. Don't want to become some needy stalker."

Laughing, he shook his head as she retracted her hand, his skin on fire where she'd touched him. "You're no such thing. I like supporting you, Jus. It's no big deal."

Her eyes were kind as she studied him, and he noticed the deep amber flecks deep within the brown orbs. Her hair was short, and she'd dyed it some pinkish color, but it looked full and gorgeous as always. She was one of those women who seemed to get prettier as they aged and grew into themselves. Her beauty had been wasted on that bastard Dean Rodgers for too long, and he was glad she was free of his toxicity. Justine was way too good for that scumbag and always had been.

"Any word from Dean?" he asked, wanting to tread lightly but unable to quelch his curiosity.

"Nope," she said, finishing her brownie and wiping her hands. "He's in love with his new flame. I hope they're happy and leave us alone forever."

"Good to hear. Nicole's getting married and moving to Virginia Beach. I'm sending my last alimony check tomorrow. Guess we're both free and clear."

"Yes, we are," she said with a determined nod. "You know what? I think that means we need to celebrate."

Gary lifted his brows. "Celebrate how?"

"Um, we need to have a party," she said as if the answer were obvious. "A *freedom* party." Lifting her arms high, she wiggled her hands in a mock cheer.

"I want to have a party!" Avery exclaimed, joining in the revelry.

"Well, there you have it. A freedom party to celebrate both of us moving the heck on."

"I don't want to make a big deal of it," he said, wrinkling his nose. "And isn't that our private business?"

"Not in Ardor Creek," she said, scrunching her features. "Everyone and their mother must know about our situations. And I bet half of them are pitying us. *Oh, poor Justine and Gary,*" she said, lifting her fist to her eye while she imitated crying. "*Hope they're okay now that their exes have moved on.* We'll show them."

"That's extremely dramatic," Gary muttered.

"We'll show them," Avery repeated with a tilt of her head.

"That's right, baby. Come on—it will be fun! We can have it in my back yard, and we'll invite the gang. We need to take advantage of the warm weather before it turns cold."

"I've been picking up a lot of overtime, so my only days off are Sundays."

"Fine, we'll do it on a Sunday. That means we'll have to invite my parents. They won't meddle or anything." She gave a sarcastic eye roll. "Anyway, I'll take care of everything. How about this Sunday?"

Gary's first inclination was to say no, but he glanced down at Avery, who was looking at him with wide, excited eyes, and he melted on the spot. "Okay, if everyone's available on Sunday, that's fine."

"I'm sure people will have to rearrange their Ardor Creek social calendars, but it can be done," Justine said sardonically.

"Yay! A party!"

"But no signs or fanfare," he said, lifting a finger. "Let's just keep it chill." Gary had always been a rather private person and a bit shy, and he didn't want his business blasted around town.

"Cancel the banner that says '*Gary's love life is now open for business*,'" Justine mused, looking at the ceiling as she tapped her finger on her chin. "Got it."

"Jus..." he warned.

"Geez, does anyone joke with you?" She winked, sending his heart into overdrive. He loved her energy and sense of humor, which balanced out his calm, pragmatic personality.

"My mom has a great sense of humor, but since she and Dad moved to Florida to play canasta full-time, not really."

Chuckling, Justine stood and collected their plates. "Noted." Striding over to the sink, she began to wash them.

"You don't have to do that," Gary said, rising and approaching her. Sliding his hand over the juncture between her neck and shoulder, he almost shivered at the softness of her skin. "I have a dishwasher, Jus."

She glanced up at him as she circled the sponge over the plate. "It's a plate, Gary. I think I can handle it."

He smiled as he stared into her eyes, telling himself to remove his hand, but the damn thing was suddenly melded to her skin. Feeling his breath hitch, he felt his stomach drop to his knees when she licked her lips.

"Gary?"

"Oh, uh, okay," he said, removing his hand and backing toward the stool. His knees were suddenly wobbly as hell, and he sat, hoping it would calm his pounding heart. "Thank you for washing it."

Justine finished and put the plate in the drying rack before asking Avery to bring over the cups. She washed those too and dried her hands before folding the towel on the counter.

"Well, I think we've tortured you enough. One spilled milk carton and three brownies later, this one needs to go to bed. What do you say to Gary, Avery?"

"Thank you for the milk," she said, giving him a blazing smile.

"You're welcome. Thank you for the brownies." Rising, he led them down the hallway to the front door, opening it before they walked outside.

"I'll tell everyone to come over at one o'clock," Justine said, facing him. "That way, you all can watch the football game inside when you need a break."

"The Steelers are playing the Jets," he said, arching a brow. "Should be a good game."

"Well, yay sports and all that jazz," she said, waving her hands back and forth. "I know nothing about football, but I hope they score a basket and hit a home run."

He gave her a droll look. "You have to know there are no baskets in football, Justine."

Laughing, she winked again, and his heart lurched in his chest. "Okay, that was too far. Obviously, I know a little bit about football. Mark and Dad are huge fans, and they forced me and Mom to watch."

"Sounds like A *Clockwork Orange*."

"It was worse," she said, lifting a brow. "Come on, baby." Extending her hand to Avery, she gave a wave before they turned and began walking down the porch stairs.

"Did you drive over?"

"We walked," she called, trailing across his yard. "It's a nice night, and it's not too far."

Nodding, Gary watched them pace down the road before he closed the door. Heading to his room, he slipped on his sneakers and padded back down the stairs. Stepping outside, he closed the door behind him and began the walk to her house. A few minutes later, he arrived, ensuring they were safe at home as he saw their silhouettes in the upstairs windows. Making sure they were safe was one thing, but he didn't want to lurk, so he turned and walked home, thankful for their visit. Once home, he began mentally preparing for the party he didn't really want to have. But Justine wanted it, and so did Avery, so he'd join the revelry if it made them happy.

Stepping inside the house, he trod to the kitchen, noting how quiet it was now that they were gone. Helping himself to one last brownie, he tidied up before finally sitting down to apply the heating pad to his thigh.

<h1 style="text-align:center">Chapter 4</h1>

The week flew by, and before Gary knew it, Sunday arrived. When he awoke that morning, he was quite nervous, which was ridiculous since he was going to be hanging out with people he'd known his whole life. He'd attended tons of his friends' barbeques and cookouts over the years, and this one shouldn't be any different. Yes, Justine had gotten some feather in her cap about celebrating their "freedom," but he knew it was really just an excuse to gather everyone together. That was fine with Gary since he hadn't seen his buddies in a while due to his busy work schedule, and he was excited to relax and have some fun.

His friends were all hitched up now and starting families of their own. Gary was glad they'd all found love and created happiness in their lives. He and Nicole had discussed having kids during their marriage, but it had never been the right time. As their relationship deteriorated, they had sex less often until it became quite infrequent. And then, he got shot, and their chances of having a kid were obliterated.

Gary's doctor had indicated there was still a small chance he could father children, but it was a long shot due to the damage to his pelvic region when the bullet erupted at the top of his inner thigh. It had injured his entire groin area, and the scar tissue significantly reduced his sperm count. Not only that, but it was pretty hard to knock up your wife when you struggled to maintain an erection.

Sighing at the unwanted and embarrassing thoughts, Gary pushed them away to focus on getting ready. He'd asked Justine if she wanted him to come over early to help set up, and she'd accepted. Once he was dressed in his casual clothes, he threw on his light jacket and walked to her house. As he approached the open front door, he heard music blasting inside.

"Jus?" he asked, peering through the front door as he knocked, although it was imperceptible beneath the loud music. "Avery?"

"Gary!" Avery yelled, running toward him and grabbing his hand. "Come on—we're having a dance party to Madonna!"

She dragged him into the living room where Justine was dancing to an upbeat song. Her body gyrated and twirled in a sexy rhythm, setting every cell of his skin on fire, and he stood frozen as Avery ran to her and joined in. They hopped and jumped, hooking their fingers as they beckoned to him.

"Come on, Gary," Justine said, waving him over. "It's 'Holiday' by Madonna. It's sacrilegious *not* to dance."

"Uh, thanks, I'm all set," he said, showing her his palms.

"No way, buster." Skipping over, she grabbed his wrists and began pulling him to the center of the room.

Gary grimaced at the pain that shot through his leg, and she halted, staring at him with remorse. "Oh, crap. Did I hurt you? Mark told me you still have some pain from when you got shot all those years ago. Damn it, I'm sorry."

"You said a curse word!" Avery shouted, still dancing.

"Moms can say curse words sometimes, but little girls can't. Got it?"

Avery nodded, and Justine faced him. "Do you want some ibuprofen or something, or...shit," she said softly so the music drowned out the bad word. "Do you want to sit down?"

What he *wanted* was not to make a big deal of it, so he smiled and shook his head. "I'm a terrible dancer, but I can try." He would probably look like the world's biggest idiot, but if it kept Justine from focusing on his injury, he didn't care. The wound had already cost him too much, and he wouldn't let it dampen their day.

"Oh, well, great!" Clasping his hand, she led him into the center of the carpeted floor. "Okay, the next song after this is 'Wake Me Up Before You Go-Go.' It's starting in three...two...one...and go!"

They moved to the upbeat song, Gary shifting his weight from one foot to the other and trying not to look like an ass. He snapped his fingers a few times, and Justine beamed. "Not bad, Officer Lincoln. You've got some moves."

He wasn't sure about that, but if dancing made her smile at him like that, he'd do it all day long and in his sleep too. God, she was so pretty, and she was wearing some pink sparkly lip gloss that sent a jolt to his crotch. It was exhilarating, and he decided he was leaving law enforcement to become a professional dancer just so he could see this exact look on her face every damn day.

Unfortunately, his dreams of becoming Fred Astaire all but vanished when Mark and Teresa stepped into the foyer with Rose situated in a carrier that Teresa held.

"Well, what do we have here?" Mark asked, walking into the room. "I don't think I've ever seen Gary dance, not even at our wedding."

"The girls asked me to, okay?" Gary said, scowling.

"Aw, don't stop," Justine said. "Dang it, Mark, we were having fun. Thanks for ruining it."

"Hey, I thought you were doing a good job, man."

"Whatever," Gary said, running his hand through his hair. "Do you want me to help set up, Jus?"

Sighing, she walked over and turned down the music. "I guess so. People will start to filter in, so let's get to it. Teresa, did you get the banner?"

"What banner?" Gary muttered.

"Man, it's too easy with you," she said, patting his shoulder. "We'll need to work on that."

Breathing a laugh, he followed her into the kitchen and helped her prepare.

After setting tons of food, soda, wine, and beer outside on the table, Gary set up some folding chairs, and Mark helped him.

"It's nice to see you two hanging out," Mark said, dusting off the seat of one of the chairs.

"I like spending time with them, Mark. Please don't make it weird." Mark was one of the few people who knew about his feelings for Justine but had never pushed him on it. He was a good friend, and Gary appreciated him not meddling...most of the time.

"I won't," he said, grabbing a beer and twisting off the cap. He handed it to Gary before opening his own. "All I'll say is she's really comfortable with you, and Avery adores you. Jus lets you in, which isn't easy for her, no matter how brave a face she shows to the world. I know you and Nicole had it rough, and Justine obviously had it rough with Dean. If any two people deserve happiness, it's you guys." Holding up his bottle, he clinked it with Gary's. "To happiness."

"To happiness," Gary said, taking a sip. "Speaking of, you and Teresa have this whole 'building a family while having thriving careers' thing down." He made quotation marks with his fingers. "How do you do it? I'm exhausted just looking at you guys."

Laughing, Mark shook his head. "We're lucky because Teresa can make her own hours. She stopped taking new patients once we decided to adopt and now only sees her established clients. The part-time schedule lets her take care of Rose while I save the world."

"Okay, Mr. D.A.," Gary teased. "Someone's getting a little big for their britches."

Mark chuckled. "Honestly, we just decided to make it work. We sat down and figured out what needed to happen to build the life we wanted. That's how you do it, I guess. Look at Carrie and Peter, Scott and Ashlyn, and Chad and Abby. We all figured it out in our own ways."

"Yeah," Gary said, staring past the swing set in Justine's back yard to the horizon in the distance. "I'm really happy for you guys. Rose is so cute."

"She's our little miracle. Thank goodness I begged Teresa to take me back and she listened. I was a huge dope. Don't be a dope with my sister, okay, man?"

"You said no meddling."

"That's it, I promise," he said, pursing his lips. "I just don't want to see you make my mistakes." Glancing around, he nodded. "I think we did a good job. We definitely deserve to turn the Steelers on and watch the first quarter until everyone gets here."

"My friend," Gary said, placing his hand on his shoulder, "lead the way."

Glad to leave any conversation about his feelings for Justine behind, Gary followed his buddy inside.

J ustine sipped her spiked seltzer and hiccupped, realizing she was tipsy. Eliciting a giggle, she swiped the back of her arm over her lips.

"Someone needs to be cut off," Carrie teased.

"Nah, I'm good," Justine said, taking another swig. "This is a celebration, right? And it's my house, so I don't have to drive anywhere. I'm letting my hair down."

"I love it," Ashlyn said, taking a sip of her wine. They were sitting in folding chairs on the patio as the men played in the yard with the kids. Avery was having a grand ol' time kicking the soccer ball with Sebastian and Charlie, and Justine reveled in her laughter.

"She's adjusted so well after the divorce, Justine," Teresa said from her spot between Carrie and Abby. "You've done an excellent job."

"I appreciate your help with all your super-spidey therapy skills," Justine said, wiggling her fingers. "You've been a godsend, Teresa. As I've always said, if my brother is dumb enough to ever fuck things up with you, I'm keeping you in the divorce."

Laughing, Teresa shook her head. "That's lovely, but hopefully, we'll be okay."

The ladies chuckled as the sun sat low on the distant horizon.

"Speaking of happily ever after," Carrie said, mischief in her tone, "you and Gary seem *very* comfortable with each other—"

"Wow. My mom made it through the entire party without grilling me before she left. I thought I was free and clear."

"What? It's just an observation."

"From the biggest gossip in town," Ashlyn muttered under her breath.

"I heard that," Carrie said, scrunching her features, "and there are several other gossips in town worse than me. I just happen to hear everything because GDC faces Main Street. People drop in all the time to give me the scoop."

"Perhaps I should designate an official title for you," Abby said, rubbing her chin. "Chief Gossip Officer of Ardor Creek."

"Thanks, Mayor Hanson, but I'm all set." She winked. "But seriously, I'm not trying to meddle, Jus—"

Ashlyn coughed loudly into her fist.

"Oh, stop it," Carrie said, swatting her. "If you weren't my best friend, I'd be pissed. Anyway, I just think you're great, and I think Gary is great, and that's all I'm saying. If you guys are friends, I don't see how it would hurt to give dating a try. He's always been so handsome and a little shy." Lifting her hand, she whispered loudly, "You know what they say about shy ones, right?"

Justine rolled her eyes. "Can't wait to hear—"

"They're awesome in bed."

"Uh, yeah, I think we got that, Carrie," Abby chimed.

Biting her lip, Carrie stared at Justine. "Sooooo...?"

Sighing, Justine crossed her arms. "Look, guys, I just don't know. I keep telling myself I have to get back out there, but it's hard, you know? Dean is the only guy I've ever been with. I'm literally the worst person in the world with relationships."

"He wasn't right for you," Teresa said. "That doesn't mean someone else won't be."

"I know." Taking a sip of her drink, she contemplated. "Gary was there the night everything went down with Dean. I sometimes wonder if he could ever see me in a romantic light. That night was so fucked up, and I still remember everything he did to help me. Maybe he just sees me as a friend."

"How will you know unless you ask him?" Ashlyn asked.

Narrowing her eyes, Justine stared at Gary as he kicked the soccer ball to Charlie. "I guess I could take being rejected. It's not as bad as getting the crap beaten out of you."

"Don't waste your energy on those thoughts, Justine," Teresa said. "It does no good to blame yourself. That part of your life is over."

"Thank god." Her throat bobbed as she mulled. "If Gary rejects me, will it make it weird? I think a part of me is scared of that. He's become such a good friend, and I don't want to fuck it up."

"There are times when you just have to go for it, Jus," Ashlyn said, shrugging. "I know it's hard. I was terrified I was awful at relationships after Robert. Scott and I aren't perfect, but it's a thousand times better with him than it ever was with my douche ex-fiancé. And now we have two kids and are living the dream." Dramatically swiping her thick black hair off her shoulder, she snickered.

"I'll think about it," Justine said, chugging the rest of her spiked seltzer before standing. "In the meantime, I have a killer buzz I don't want to waste. Anyone interested in joining the kids so I can show you how dreadful I am at soccer?"

"I'm in," Ashlyn said, rising. "Let's do this."

"Ladies?"

"I'm fine with my wine," Carrie said, saluting her. "Tell Peter to tire the boys out as much as possible. All this talk of true love has me excited to get the kids to bed early tonight so we can have our own playtime." She waggled her eyebrows.

Chuckling, Justine gave a salute. "Done." She and Ashlyn jogged over to join the others. Gary smiled as she approached, sending a nervous jolt of awareness through her frame. Heeding her friends' words, Justine decided she would try to make a move if the opportunity presented itself. She was certainly no femme fatale, but she didn't want to live as someone scared or timid. She'd grown brave about pursuing her dream of being an artist and felt she could also channel that energy into her love life.

Would Gary reject her? Would it change things between them? She had no idea but didn't want to waste time worrying about the outcome of chances she hadn't even taken. Edging closer, she tapped him on the shoulder.

"Do you mind helping me clean up before you walk home?"

"I was already planning on it," he said with a nod.

"Awesome. Now, let me show you how terrible I am at sports. Get ready."

His warm chuckle surrounded her as she trailed toward the soccer ball and kicked it straight into the bush. Oh yeah, she was awful, but for some reason, Gary's smile made her feel like a goddamn Olympic athlete.

Chapter 5

E ventually, the sun set, and everyone gathered the kids to head home. Gary informed Justine he'd clean up while she put Avery to bed, and the sweet offer only reinforced her decision to explore something more between them. Nerves flitted in her stomach along with anticipation as she read a book to Avery once she was tucked in. When her eyes began to droop, Justine kissed her on the forehead and flicked off the light, leaving the door open just a crack as Avery preferred.

Once downstairs, she searched for Gary, finding him on the back porch wiping down the long table.

"Hey," he said, swishing the rag over the far corner. "Everything's all packaged up in containers in the fridge. The leftover sodas and beers are in the cooler, which I emptied."

"Wow," she said, stepping closer and sliding her hands into the back pockets of her jeans. "You're hired. Do you do windows too?"

Breathing a laugh, he fiddled with the cloth as his eyes darted to hers. He seemed slightly nervous, causing her to wonder if his thoughts were drifting the same way as hers. "I'd consider it for an extra fee."

Arching a brow, she said, "Name your price."

His gaze dropped to her lips, jump-starting her heartbeat as they stood under the stars. Unconsciously, her tongue darted out to lick them, and she noticed the flare of arousal in his deep brown eyes. Fear gripped her as she stood frozen, debating if this was the time to make a move.

"I...uh...well, I should probably get home," he said, effectively dousing her plan. "Unless you need something else cleaned?"

Laughing, she shook her head. "Nope. Am I an ass for making you clean up at your own party? I think I am."

"Never." He gave a quick wink, and Justine felt her heart drop to her knees. Realizing she wasn't ready to let him go yet, she tilted her head. "Can you stay and have one more drink with me? I promise you won't have to do any manual labor."

"Sure."

Gesturing him inside, she directed him to the kitchen sink, where they washed their hands, and she grabbed two cans from the fridge. "Beer's okay, right?"

"Yep." Taking it, he flipped the can open and saluted. "To a successful party."

"To our freedom," she said, clinking her can against his. "How are you feeling about that, by the way?"

"About my freedom?"

Nodding, she began walking toward the living room, and he fell into step beside her.

"Good, I guess. I'm happy that Nicole is happy."

They sat on each end of the couch as the dim light of the lamp shone over them. "That's pretty awesome. I think a part of me wishes Dean won't find happiness. God, that's awful, isn't it? Forget I said it. Yikes."

"It's not awful, Jus," he said, shaking his head. "He wasn't a good man. I'm happy you were able to leave him."

"It took me too long," she said, frowning. "I told myself I loved him, but that wasn't really love. It was so fucking toxic. I'm happy to be free, but I do miss having a companion, you know?"

His throat bobbed as he contemplated. "I guess. I'm not sure if Nicole and I were ever really partners. I kind of like flying solo. Less complicated."

Feeling her eyebrows draw together, she scooted closer. "Don't you get lonely though?"

Lifting a shoulder, he shrugged. "Not really. There are...expectations that come along with being in a relationship, and I'm just not sure I'm ready for those."

Justine gnawed her lip, wondering what expectations he was worried about. From what she knew of Gary, he was a lovely, thoughtful man who would be an amazing partner. Curiosity welled deep within as he took another swig of his beer.

"I get lonely sometimes," she said, running her fingers over the smooth fabric of the sofa. "I miss being held. Being loved. Maybe that's needy, but it's just how I feel."

"That's perfectly normal. I have no doubt you'll find someone you deserve one day. Someone who will fit with you and Avery, and who can make you happy."

Emotion swamped her, perhaps enhanced by the alcohol she'd imbibed throughout the day, and tears welled in her eyes. He obviously didn't see himself as a candidate for the man who would eventually be her partner. Was it because of her history with Dean? Or the disastrous night she'd been arrested for attempted murder? Before she could ask him, he cleared his throat and stood.

"Well, I've got to be at the station at seven tomorrow. Guess I should be heading home." Lifting the can to his lips, he took a hefty sip before setting it on the side table. "Thanks for the drink."

"Sure," she said, rising. She walked him to the foyer and stuck her hands in her pockets as he donned his jacket.

"I had a good time. Thanks for inviting me to the party I didn't want to have."

A laugh escaped her lips. "You're welcome. Thanks for letting me force it down your throat."

His eyes sparkled as he grinned. "It wasn't that bad. Have a good week, Jus." Facing the door, he encircled the knob and pulled it open.

"I have a show at the gallery on Friday," she said, scrambling to find an excuse to see him again. "If you want to stop by."

"I'd love that. I'm also going to karaoke with the gang on Wednesday, if you want to come. Peter roped me into it tonight while we were playing with the kids. Kara is going to babysit for them, and I'm sure she'd watch Avery too."

"Ohh, sounds fun. I'll let you know, but I should be able to. Thanks for the invite."

"Sure thing." With a final wave, he turned and trailed through the door, his broad shoulders visible as he walked through her yard and eventually disappeared.

Closing the door, she locked the deadbolt and rested her palm flat against the wood. Running her free hand over her face, she blew a breath through her lips. "He's not interested, Jus. It's obvious he just wants to be friends. Leave it alone."

Sighing, she grabbed their cans from the living room and snapped off the lamp before tidying up the kitchen. After prepping for bed, she lay beneath the soft covers, her mind racing as she contemplated. Although she was trying to convince herself Gary wasn't interested, her mind kept replaying that one moment they'd stood in the moonlight as she licked her lips. The desire in his eyes had been unmistakable, and that gave her a tiny spark of hope.

Could two people with such terrible relationship histories even begin to make something work? Justine wasn't sure, but she knew one thing: She wasn't ready to give up. Gary was a tough nut to crack, but she had always been stubborn. Her parents would attest to that all day long and twice on Sunday. So, she'd study her handsome friend and do her best to figure out what was holding him back. If he didn't want to chance messing up their friendship, Justine would accept that, but something about it didn't seem right. No, she had a feeling there was something else dictating his actions.

Determined to figure it out, Justine mulled long into the night until she succumbed to sleep.

Gary entered his house, besieged by swirling thoughts as his head pounded. It was most likely from the recent beer, which he'd all but chugged once Justine began talking about being lonely. Emitting a frustrated huff, he hung his jacket on the rack and padded to the living room. Lowering onto the couch, he rested his face in his hands, spearing his fingers through his hair as his elbows rested on his thighs. Slightly rocking back and forth, he muttered, "Don't go there, Gary. You'll set yourself up for disaster."

Although he hated remembering the awful fights he'd had with Nicole, the memories rushed in. Annoyed, he sat back on the couch and rubbed his eyes. Hell, if he was going to take a trip down memory lane, he might as well immerse himself in it, if only as a reminder of why he would never allow his relationship with Justine to turn romantic.

Sinking into the couch, he squeezed his eyes as the memory of their last terrible fight took hold.

"What the hell, Gary?" Nicole yelled, pushing him away as she sat up on the bed. "Again? Is it me? Do you not want me anymore?"

Guilt, frustration and sadness all swirled together as he assessed her angry expression. "It's not you, Nicole. I'm trying here, okay?"

"The doctor said you should be fine if you're aroused," she said, rising and grabbing her robe from the hook on the closet door before shrugging it on. "So, either you don't want me or you're just not into having sex anymore, and I'm not going to live like that, Gary."

"What do you suggest, Nicole?" he yelled, rising and jerking on his underwear. "I can't fucking control it. I got shot in a major vessel, for Christ's sake. Do you even care?"

"Of course I care, but I'm not going to sign up for a life without sex. We're in our thirties, Gary. If we're lucky, we have decades left. Decades! Can you really go the rest of your life without intimacy?"

"Sex isn't intimacy, Nicole. If you weren't so damn hard on me, this would probably be easier. I want to be intimate with you, but your expectations create a ton of anxiety."

"Oh, so it's my fault?"

"Of course it's not your fault, but there are some things I can't control. We made a promise to love each other through sickness and health. That means something to me. I need you to have a little compassion here."

Her chin warbled as she swiped a tear away. "We were so young when we got married," she almost whispered.

"What are you saying, Nicole?"

She covered her mouth, her eyes red as she stared at him.

"Just say it. Let's finally start being honest with each other."

A sob leaped from her throat. "I can't do this, Gary. Sex has always been our connector. The one thing we counted on when nothing else worked. And now..." Lifting her hands, she shook her head. "Now, that's gone too. I can't do this if we can't connect that way. I'm sorry."

His gaze trailed to the floor, resting on the soft carpet as he searched for something to latch onto in his dying marriage. Unfortunately, the woven strands held no answers. Focusing on her, he sighed. "Don't give up on us, Nicole. I'll go back to the doctor. Maybe there's something else he can do."

Pursing her lips, she gave a slight nod. "Okay. I'll give you time, but I can't give you forever, Gary. Not if we can't figure this out."

"Okay," he said, rubbing his forehead. "I'm going to sleep on the couch. I think it's best if we both clear our heads."

"Fine," she said, her tone cold.

Gary had stormed out of the room, grabbing a t-shirt from the dresser before heading downstairs for a sleepless night on the couch. After that night, he'd never touched Nicole again, although he hadn't known at the time it would be their last attempt at intimacy. Gary had visited several specialists in Scranton, all of whom plied him with various erectile dysfunction prescriptions and suggested other options such as injections in his nether region, which he wasn't really keen on trying. In the end, the damage had already been done.

Several weeks later, Gary was called to the town pub on Main Street to assess a drunk and disorderly call. When he walked inside, he broke up a fight between two men he hadn't previously seen in Ardor Creek. Eventually, he took down their information and recognized one of their names.

"Jerry Northam," Gary said, handing him back his license. "I think you run the gym where my wife has recently been taking yoga in Battle Falls."

The man gazed at him with glassy eyes. "Yoga," he drawled. "Is that what she told you we've been doing?"

Gary always thought he'd feel rage if he ever found out Nicole had cheated, but at that moment, all he felt was sadness. There in the bar on Main Street, he realized once and for all his marriage was over.

When he returned home that evening, Nicole met him in the foyer.

"Lauren called," she said softly, referencing her longtime friend. She appeared contrite, which only affirmed her guilt. "She told me about the fight at the pub."

"I never thought you'd do it, Nicole," he said, turning to place his duty belt on the table. It gave him a mundane task to focus on as the sadness and anger churned inside.

"I told you, Gary," she rasped, emotion lacing the words. "I can't do this anymore. It's over."

He nodded, setting the last of his equipment on the table before resting his palms flat. Unable to look her in the eye, he spoke in a droll tone. "I'll have Mark recommend a divorce lawyer. You should find one too."

"Okay." Silence permeated the room as she inched closer and gently rested her hand on his shoulder. "I'm so sorry."

Closing his eyes to block out the pain, he sighed. "Me too, Nicole."

They'd stood there for several minutes, both acknowledging the demise of their marriage, before she packed a bag and decided to stay with Lauren. And just like that, his marriage had been toast.

Now, sitting on the couch in the dim living room, Gary let the pain and grief simmer. It was a visible reminder that he had no business pursuing a romantic relationship with anyone, especially Justine who deserved someone who could love her fully. The thought of disappointing her if they tried to make love was too much to fathom.

Gary's prognosis after his injury had been vague at best. The physicians all assured him he would be able to maintain and sustain erections in certain situations. The doctors were clear that the more comfortable he felt with a partner, the easier it would be for his body to perform sexually. Sex with Nicole had been tough because their marriage was already strained before his injury. Afterward, Gary felt pressure to perform, knowing it was the one thing that sustained their relationship and, ironically, that had most likely led to his lackluster performance.

Justine didn't deserve being saddled with someone who couldn't please her. Hell, he'd probably just dig himself a great big hole and burrow inside forever if he let her down. No, it was easier to remain friends. Pursuing a romantic relationship would only lead to heartache, and they'd both had too much of that already.

Running his fingers through his hair, he resolved to remain firm in his decision. When Justine looked at him with those sparkling eyes and pretty lips, he would secretly admire her while pushing his feelings away. Maybe he could even set her up with someone else. Frowning, he realized that might be a bit too far. After all, there was only so much torture a man could take. Still, he wanted her to be happy and hated that she was lonely. Hopefully, one day, she would find someone worthy of her and Avery. In another world, that man would be him, but Gary lived in the real world, and the time for daydreams had long passed.

Realizing his head was now fully pounding, he stood and headed to the bathroom to pop some aspirin before bed.

Chapter 6

T he week was busy for Justine as she juggled her daily routine of being a single mom, preparing for Friday's showcase, and making progress on the sculpture she was perfecting. Her studio was located in a shed in her back yard she'd hired Scott Grillo to build years ago. Justine had a feeling he'd vastly undercharged her, but he and Mark were good friends and that was the way of small towns. She absolutely adored the space, and it was big enough for her pottery wheel, canvases, and other materials.

Justine had always been bitten by the creative bug and felt extremely lucky she could express herself through her art. Having the ability to paint and sculpt brought her pleasure in a life that had sometimes been anything but fulfilling. Now that she was free from her abusive marriage, every day of her newfound life with Avery was a gift.

On Wednesday morning, she worked on her new sculpture for a few hours before stepping outside to inhale the fresh fall air. Her ears perked as she heard a shrill, steady beeping in the distance, and she trailed along the fence that separated her yard from the house next door to explore.

Sure enough, a midsize moving truck was backing into the driveway. The house next door had been vacant ever since the owners sold it and retired to Georgia. Curious, Justine wiped her hands on her jeans as she observed a man exit the truck and walk around the back to slide open the door.

"Are you moving in?" she called, approaching as the man whirled and placed his hand over his heart.

"Damn, you scared me," he said, expelling a breath. "Yes, I closed last week and will be slowly moving in over the next week."

"Well, we're neighbors then," she said, extending her hand. "Sorry for the scare. I'm pretty nosy, so it's best to get that out in the open, I guess. Justine Lancaster."

Chuckling, he shook. "Jeremy Kramer. Nice to meet you."

"Welcome to Ardor Creek. It's annoying and awesome, both at once. I've lived here my whole life, so if you need anything, just let me know."

"Thanks. I'm relocating from Philly. I'm an author, so I can work anywhere, which is nice."

"Ohh, an author. Anything I might have heard of?"

He grinned. "Not sure. Do you read sci-fi? My best-selling book is called *Alternate Destinies*."

"Wait," she said, eyes growing wide. "You're J.R. Kramer? I read Alternate Destinies last year and loved it. All the time travel and parallel universes? They were awesome. Like, they were confusing but made sense all at the same time."

"Well, I'm glad you liked it. The sales on that one allowed me to afford this lovely little home," he said, gesturing to the two-bedroom house. "And now, I just have to write ten more bestsellers to send my girls to college."

"You have daughters?"

"Twin girls," he said with a nod. "Eight years old, going on forty."

Justine belted a laugh. "I've got a seven-year-old who's exactly the same. She's wise and is sure to tell everyone about it. And I hear you on the college racket." She rolled her eyes. "I save as much as I can in Avery's college fund, but she's going to be getting scholarships. Mark my words."

"I hear that. Hopefully, my girls will do the same. Lord knows, it would save me a fortune."

Feeling curious, Justine craned her neck. "Is there a Mrs. J.R. Kramer?" She bit her lip, hoping she wasn't being rude.

"There was once, but we decided it was best if we lived the rest of our lives as friends and co-parents. She actually grew up in Battle Falls and moved back after our divorce. We share custody of the girls and were getting tired of shuffling back and forth. Both of my parents passed away over the past year, so there was no reason for me to stay in Philly."

"I'm so sorry to hear that." Compassion swelled as she imagined losing both of her parents in the span of a year. They were both annoying at times, but she loved them dearly. "That must've been really hard."

"It was," he said, resting his hands on his hips. "Makes you remember what's important in life."

"So true. Well, I'll let you get back to it. I'm an artist and my studio is in the back yard, so if you see me tinkering around, that's what I'm doing."

"Wow, now I'm impressed. You paint?"

"Yep. And sculpt too. It's the only thing I've ever wanted to do."

"Well, I hope to see your work someday. Do you do showings?"

"I have one this Friday, actually, at the one and only gallery in Ardor Creek. It's a bastion of refined elegance right in the middle of Main Street," she teased, wrinkling her nose.

"Jenny has the girls on Friday," he said, rubbing his chin. "Maybe I'll stop by. I guess Friday is as good a time as any to familiarize myself with Main Street."

"You'll learn it in a day, believe me. I'll drop a flyer in your mailbox so you have the info. Nice to meet you, Jeremy."

"Nice to meet you too."

Waving, Justine headed back to her shed, thrilled to have met a famous author—one who was now her neighbor. Excitement roared inside as she realized she was aching to tell someone. Grabbing her phone from her pocket, she pulled up her contacts and began to scroll through. She could call Mark or Teresa, but before she knew it, her fingers had pulled up Gary's number. Deciding to go with it, she pressed the number and lifted the phone to her ear.

"Jus?" his baritone chimed, surrounding her like a warm blanket. "You okay?"

"Yeah, sorry to bother you. Are you arresting someone?"

His chuckle traveled through the phone, causing her to close her eyes and imagine him making the sound against the shell of her ear. Was Gary someone who would laugh as he made love?

Would he tease and show playful affection? It was something she'd rarely experienced with Dean, and she had the feeling sex with Gary would be an entirely different ballgame.

"I'm just sitting in my patrol car behind Vance Appliances. Just another quiet day in Ardor Creek. How are you?"

"I'm good. Tell me you've heard of J.R. Kramer."

"The guy who wrote *Alternate Destines*?"

"Yes! Gary, you won't believe this. He's my new neighbor. He's moving into the Robinsons' old house."

"No way. That's pretty cool! I really enjoyed his book. Listened to the audio sometimes in the car when it was slow at night. I also listened to *The Millennium Paradox*."

"Oh, I read that one too. So freaking good. I invited him to the gallery show on Friday. He seems nice and has two daughters close to Avery's age. He's also divorced."

"Damn, Jus. Did you get his social security number too?"

Laughing, she shook her head. "I informed him right away that I'm extremely nosy. He seemed fine with it. Anyway, I had to tell someone, and my fingers couldn't find your number fast enough."

A pause stretched before he cleared his throat. "Well, I'm happy you wanted to tell me. You and I will be the only people in Ardor Creek who know for at least an hour."

She breathed a laugh. "Yep. It will be all over town before we know it." Longing to extend their conversation, she kicked the ground with the toe of her sneaker. "I'm going to karaoke tonight. Kara is going to watch Avery at Peter's. Thanks for inviting me."

"You're always welcome, hon. I pretty much detest karaoke, but Peter was persuasive."

Justine smiled at the endearment, allowing the jolt from hearing it in his deep voice to wash over her.

"Did I lose you?" he asked after a few seconds. "Sorry. Didn't mean to call you that. It slipped."

"I liked it," she said softly. "You can call me that anytime you want."

A slow breath traveled over the phone, and she swore she felt it against her skin. "Well, I'd better get back to work."

"Oh, um, yeah. Me too. I'm working on a sculpture that I kind of love. I'll show it to you next time you come over."

"I'd love to see it. Thanks for calling, Jus."

"See you tonight."

"See ya."

Clicking off the phone, she held it to her chest, unable to deny the rapid beating of her heart. If talking on the phone to Gary elicited this type of response, what would happen if they kissed? Would he moan in that deep baritone as his tongue slid over hers? Dying to find out, Justine headed to her shed and resumed working while she mentally took inventory of her closet, deciding she would wear something that would knock his socks off at the pub.

Gary's shift finished at seven, and he drove home to change before heading to the pub. Once dressed in his favorite jeans, polo shirt, and sneakers, he called Justine to see if she needed a ride.

"Oh, sure," she said, sounding breathless over the phone. "I was late dropping Avery off, and now I'm late getting ready. I swore I was going to be on time for once tonight. Damn it."

"I think we'll survive if we miss one of Carrie and Peter's duets," he teased. "Be at your house in ten minutes—unless you need longer?"

"Nope. Give me a cutoff. I need it. See you soon."

When he arrived at her house, she appeared on the front porch, and Gary swore his eyeballs almost popped from his head. She was wearing some sort of leather skin-tight pants and a bright pink blouse that brought out the rose gold shade in her short hair. Her heels were also a pinkish color, and lascivious visions flooded his brain. Images of him holding her sexy legs high as she sprawled on his bed wearing nothing but those damn heels as he fucked her deep and hard. Justine on a normal day was absolutely gorgeous. Justine in those fucking pants and heels was a wet dream come true. Surprised at the hardening inside his jeans, he shifted in the seat as she opened the passenger door.

"Hi," she said, straightening and spreading her hands wide. "Is it too much? I don't get many adults-only nights."

"You look amazing, Jus." Noting the gravelly tone of his voice, he cleared his throat. "You'll be the prettiest woman at the pub."

"Aw," she said, sliding inside. "Thank you. I'm fine with just being the woman who doesn't have dried clay or macaroni and cheese smeared on her shirt."

Tossing back his head, he gave a hearty laugh. "Fair enough." Putting the car into drive, he fell into conversation with her, acknowledging how easy it was to just *be* with her. They had the comradery of old friends and a comfortability Gary rarely felt with anyone else.

After parking behind the pub, they entered to the sound of Ashlyn belting out an old Motown tune.

"Man, she's good," Justine said, grinning as she stared up at him. She was several inches shorter, spurring a protective streak deep within. "Let's get a drink. There's no way I can function at karaoke without some level of inebriation."

Placing his hand on the small of her back, he led her to the bar. The tips of his fingers brushed the leather at the waist of her pants, and he damn near felt his eyes cross. The urge to slide his hand down and grip the firm flesh of her ass beckoned, and he told himself to stop being a creep. Easing up to the bar, they smiled at Terry, the regular bartender and a fellow Ardor Creek lifer.

"Well, look what the cat dragged in," Terry said with a bright smile. "You look like a million bucks, Justine."

"Thanks, Terry. Must be my hot date." She winked at Gary.

"Is that so?" Terry arched a brow.

"Just the designated driver," he said, feeling slightly uncomfortable. As much as he loved spending time with Justine, he didn't want to set the rumor mill ablaze, especially since he'd decided they should stay in the friend zone. "I'll have a Diet Coke."

"Vodka soda for me," Justine said.

"Coming right up," Terry said with a nod before trailing away.

"Sorry if I made it weird," Justine said, tilting her head as her light brown eyes shimmered from the strobe light whirling above. "I know you only offered to drive me because we're neighbors. It was nice. No more 'date talk,'" she said, making quotation marks with her fingers.

Gary had to tamp down the reflexive laugh that threatened to bound from his throat. If she only knew. If things were different and he didn't have the fallout from his injury, he'd latch onto her and never let go. But life had other plans, and he wouldn't saddle her with his issues.

"You know I think you're amazing, right, Jus?"

"Um, yeah. Attempted murderess who stayed way too long with her douchelord ex. I'm a real catch." Terry appeared with their drinks, and she drew hers close, squeezing the lime into the clear liquid. "Let's move on. I don't want to ruin a fun night talking about my terrible life decisions." Lifting her glass, she clanked it with his. "Cheers."

"Cheers."

Eventually, they drifted toward the front of the room to join Ashlyn, Scott, Carrie, Peter, and Abby. "Where's Chad?" Justine asked once they were seated at the square table.

"He's in Harrisburg until Friday. The election is coming up in November, and he's working his little butt off to ensure he becomes state senator of our lovely district." She gestured around the room as Justine laughed. "I couldn't campaign with him this week because we have an important town forum tomorrow I need to be prepared for."

"Nice. The state senator and the mayor. It's like a cute rom-com or something."

"I'll let you know when Netflix calls me to buy the rights," Abby teased, playfully rolling her eyes. "Donald and Mrs. C. are babysitting Zoey and couldn't get rid of me fast enough."

"Ah, the doting grandparents. I love my parents, but they'll always be most valuable to me as free babysitters," she said, lifting a finger.

"Truth," Abby said with a nod.

Gary watched their interplay and found himself wondering if Justine wanted more children. She was five years younger than him and had time to consider it. She was an excellent mother, and Avery was adorable. It wasn't a far-off notion she would want more.

Gary's ability to have children was something else that was extremely nebulous after his injury. The damage to his groin area had resulted in a lower sperm count, which diminished his chances of naturally conceiving. However, his physicians were optimistic he could still have children, although it might require non-traditional methods. It was one more obstacle toward building a new relationship with anyone, and if Justine wanted more children, it was another reason for him to keep his distance.

"Earth to Gary," she said, waving her hand in front of his face. "Don't pretend you didn't hear me ask you to dance. It's either you or Smitty, and I think he's already half-asleep at the bar." She pointed toward the white-haired man who was a fixture at the pub. "If you don't dance with me, I will have worn these uncomfortable shoes for nothing."

"If they're uncomfortable, how are you going to dance?" he asked, glancing at her shoes.

"Because you're going to lead." Standing, she extended her hand. "Come on. Carrie and Peter won't be duetting forever."

Sighing, he took her hand and led her onto the small floor beside the stage. Carrie's eyes lit up, and she waved as she belted the tune beside her husband. Drawing Justine close, Gary slid his arm around her waist, feeling his body harden as his fingers brushed the leather of those sexy-as-hell pants. Holding her other hand high, he grinned as she beamed up at him.

"I know you hate to dance," she whispered conspiratorially. "Thank you for humoring me."

"I like dancing with *you*, Jus. You make it fun."

He felt like the luckiest man in the world as she gazed up at him while their bodies swayed. Although he couldn't have her, for this one moment, he'd hold her close and enjoy the feel of her in his arms. Gary had lived long enough to realize small bursts of joy needed to be cherished.

"What are you thinking?" she asked softly.

His eyes darted over her face as he debated telling her everything. That he wished things were different. That he wished he'd never been shot. *That he loved her.*

"I'm anticipating how much it will hurt if you stab me in the toe with your heel while we're dancing."

Tossing her head back, she broke into joyful laughter. The skin of her throat glistened in the dim light, and Gary felt a moment of true peace. Holding her close, they swayed until Carrie and Peter finished their song.

"What did you guys think?" Carrie asked, stepping off the stage. "Peter's pretty good at that one, right?"

"Pretty good?" Peter asked, feigning offense. "I'm better than the original singer. Mickey Mouse or whatever his name is."

"Mikky Ekko," Carrie corrected, swatting his shoulder. "And let's chill with the ego, hmm? It's already too big as it is."

"You love it, woman." Leaning down, he smacked a kiss on her lips. "You love my big ego and my big—"

"Okaaaaaaay," Ashlyn interrupted, encircling Carrie's arm and tugging her away from Peter. "Before things turn X-rated, I need to pick a duet with Carrie. Come on—let's look at the book."

"Carrie adores my X-rated banter," Peter said, waggling his eyebrows. "She can't control herself when I whisper it in her ear—"

"Shut it, Peter Stratford," Carrie called as Ashlyn dragged her away. "Or I'm pulling out the comfy sweatpants when we get home."

"I'd cool it, dude," Scott said, returning from the bar and grimacing at Peter. "When Ashlyn pulls out the sweatpants, I know sex is off the table for the night."

"I heard that!" Ashlyn said, shooting him a glare.

"Love you, dear," Scott said, blowing her a kiss.

She scowled before resuming her search in the songbook.

"Wow, you all are making me reconsider dating again. I absolutely love my comfy sweatpants," Justine said.

"Oh, Care Bear knows I'm going to burn those damn sweatpants one day. She'll never see it coming." They chuckled before Peter shook his head. "Honestly, they're actually really cute on her, and I love teasing her about them. Don't tell her, okay?"

"I think she already knows," Justine said, pointing at Carrie as she shot Peter a goofy smile.

"Busted." Peter took a sip of his iced tea. "Are you two going to sing? There are a ton of duets in the songbook."

"Um, yeah, I have no desire to burst anyone's eardrums, thank you very much," Justine said. "Unless Gary agrees to sing. Then, I'll take a stab at it."

"Never gonna happen," he said, shaking his head. "You all have known me your whole lives and know damn well I'm not singing karaoke."

"Well, then, my dreams of being Mariah are dashed," she replied, dramatically resting the back of her hand on her forehead. "But I did get Gary to dance with me, so I'll take the win."

"Carrie and I are going to do another slow one later, if you all want to dance again."

Justine smiled, hope simmering in her eyes, and Gary nodded. "I'll dance one more with you." How could he not? It was impossible to say no when she gazed up at him with those luminous eyes.

When the song rolled around, Gary led her to the dance floor and held her closer this time, inhaling the fragrant scent of her hair as he reveled in her proximity.

Eventually, the night wore down, and it was time to head home.

"I had so much fun tonight," Justine said from the passenger seat as they neared her house. "Thank you for coming with me. Or for driving. I guess you weren't really *with* me, but you know what I mean."

"I enjoy hanging out with you, Jus," he said, pulling into her driveway and placing the car in park. "It was fun."

Resting her head on the seat, she turned to look at him. She'd slathered on gloss as he drove and her lips sparkled as he struggled to breathe.

"Do you want to come in? Kara will be here with Avery in a few minutes. We can have a beer while I wait for her."

Swallowing, he debated. He wanted nothing more than to come inside and spend more time with her, but that wasn't conducive to his plan to remain just friends. Holding her tonight had stirred up some pretty intense feelings, and he worried he might do something brash, like try to kiss her, if he went inside.

"I think I'm just going to head home. I have to be at the station early."

"Okay." Her eyes drifted over his features, slow and contemplative. "I wish I hadn't involved you in all my shit with Dean. I can't imagine how you must see me. How weak I must seem to you for staying with him. I wish I could change it."

"Jus," he whispered, feeling his eyebrows draw together. "I don't see you as weak. You're one of the strongest people I know. You gathered the courage to leave him even though it must've been so hard, especially since he's Avery's father. And you're such a good mom, hon. I think you're amazing."

Her eyes glistened in the moonlight, and he fought the urge to draw her into his arms. Instead, he reached over and ran the backs of his fingers over the soft skin of her cheek. "Don't cry, Jus."

"I've made so many mistakes," she whispered. "And now, I have to live with the repercussions for the rest of my damn life."

Hurting for her, he wished he could draw her pain inside his own body. He didn't understand why she was suddenly doubting herself and wanted to reassure her. Opening his mouth to speak, he turned his head when lights flashed across the driveway.

"That's Kara," she said, sighing and shaking her head. "Perfect timing, huh?"

Breathing a laugh, he dropped his hand and smiled. "Always."

"Thanks for tonight, Gary. I felt normal for a little while, and most of that was because of you. I'm really glad we're friends."

"Me too, Jus."

Reaching for the handle, she opened the door and stepped out of the car. Gary stepped out too, wanting to make sure they were locked inside safe and sound before he left. Kara hopped out of her car and waved before opening the back door. Justine bent down and reached inside, lifting Avery in her arms. The sleepy little girl wrapped her legs around Justine's waist and buried her face in her neck. Justine smoothed her blond hair as she spoke to Kara, assuring her she would Venmo her when she got inside.

Kara lowered back into her car and drove away as Justine walked toward the house.

"Good night," she whispered loudly as she held her sleeping daughter.

"Night, Jus."

Gary waited to hear the clicking of the locks before he sat behind the wheel and drove home.

Chapter 7

♥

By the time Friday rolled around, Justine was a ball of nerves, as she usually was before a showing. She was confident in her art and extremely proud of it, but Ardor Creek wasn't necessarily the best market for fine art. Still, Kristoff Van Dam was a marketing genius with a ton of connections, and Justine was sure the gallery would be packed for the showcase.

She dressed in an elegant black dress and heels, her usual attire for a showing, and fastened her pearl earrings before arranging her hair one last time. It sat full and thick in its short cut, and she loved the rose gold color. She'd been contemplating dying it light blue but hadn't gotten around to it. Self-care was tough when you were a single mom and a working artist.

She had managed to shave her legs earlier, and she grinned at her reflection as she patted herself on the back. "Way to go, Jus. You have smooth legs for absolutely zero men to touch."

Snickering, she brushed one last tint of blush across her cheeks and headed downstairs. Avery was with her parents who had offered to keep her for the night. That was fine with Justine since they could bring her by the gallery early and then put her to bed at her regularly scheduled time. Kristoff kept the gallery open late, and she didn't anticipate being done before eleven.

After stuffing everything into her black clutch, she locked the front door and hopped into her car to take the five-minute drive to Main Street. Once there, she headed inside, noticing she had half an hour to make sure everything was perfect before the gallery opened at six o'clock. Striding into the room, she smiled at Gia, the gallery associate Kristoff had hired.

"Hey, Gia, how's it going?"

"Great," the young woman said, smiling. "I have everything placed where you and Kristoff requested if you want to look around."

"Thanks." Trailing around the gallery, Justine observed the pieces, swapping two of the sculptures but mostly leaving everything in place. She had ten sculptures, fifteen paintings, and various pieces of pottery she'd designed with her pottery wheel. She enjoyed creating vases, dishes, and various other items and painting them with intricate designs. They afforded her extra income with customers who weren't in the market for fine art. After the final walk through, she approached the sales counter where Gia was waiting with a glass of champagne.

"You look like you need this."

"You're a saint," she said, taking the glass and swallowing a huge gulp. "I can't believe I still get nervous at these things."

"It's hard to put your art out there," Gia said, shrugging. "One day, I'd love to display my paintings. I'm terrified though."

"Your work is fantastic, Gia," Justine said, recalling the pieces she'd shown her one evening on her phone. "I'll talk to Kristoff about including some of your work in our next show."

"Really? That would be awesome."

"Absolutely. Just remember me when you're famous, okay?"

"I wish."

Chuckling, Justine sipped the champagne before a gregarious voice chimed, "Darling! There you are."

"Hello, Kristoff," she said, turning to face her friend. He enveloped her in a tight hug as she laughed. "Don't strangle me before the night is over. I need the dough from this show."

Drawing back, he cupped her arms. "You're going to have a marvelous night. I feel it."

"Fingers crossed." Holding them up, she grinned. "Where's Frederik?"

"Oh, he's sick, darling. Honestly, I think he just doesn't want to leave the city, and we got in a terrible fight about it."

"I'm sorry. I'm guessing he's not a fan of our quaint little town."

"He's a New Yorker for life," Kristoff said, swinging a dismissive hand through the air. "But I've fallen in love with Ardor Creek and adore the little country house we bought here."

"I'm not sure four bedrooms is *little*," she chided, sipping her drink.

"Oh, you know what I mean. Anyway, my husband will come around eventually. Tonight is about you. Let's sell the shit out of your art so I can go home tomorrow and tell Frederik he missed a terribly exciting evening."

Laughing, she nodded. "I'm ready."

The front door swung open, and before Justine knew it, the gallery was packed. She did her best to interact with the patrons, hoping the personal touch would help open their wallets. At one point, she approached a woman who was gazing at one of her paintings of the lake that sat by the reservoir on the outskirts of town.

"It's from one of our local lakes," Justine said. "It's one of my favorite spots in town."

"I know," the woman said, her tone slightly morose. "I remember it."

Justine's eyebrows drew together as she tried to place the woman. She looked slightly familiar, but she couldn't quite put her finger on it. "Are you from Ardor Creek?"

Fully facing her, the woman shot her an annoyed glare. "Yes. I was in your brother's grade. He and his perfect friends didn't run in the same circles as I did. I was more the 'mean cheerleader' type, if you catch my drift."

"Heather Combs?" Justine asked, finally recognizing her. She had been somewhat of a legend back in the day. The prettiest girl in school—and the bitchiest, from what Justine remembered. Even though she'd been five years older, Heather Combs' reputation had a far reach.

"I thought you moved out of Ardor Creek once you and Butch divorced."

"I did. And now he's marrying Cynthia Andrews, who couldn't keep her legs closed even if someone bolted a chastity belt on her. What a floozy. I'm back now, and they can both deal with it."

Justine pursed her lips, unsure of what to say. She'd met Cynthia a few times and wasn't really a fan, but she didn't feel the need to bash the woman.

"I know, I'm a bitch for saying it. Once a bitch, always a bitch, right? Might as well live up to my squalid reputation." She rolled her eyes.

"Well, I don't really have an opinion on that since I don't know you, but I'm happy you're at my showcase. If you want the painting, I'll be happy to give you an extra ten percent off as a welcome back gift."

Tilting her head, Heather assessed her. "You're nice. Your brother was too. I didn't really hate his crew...well, except for Abby. She rubbed me the wrong way. Chad Hanson insisted on being her friend, and I just didn't get it since she was a pariah. And now, she's mayor, and they're married. Karma really is something, huh? They're happy as shit, and I'm a divorced tramp who just moved back to the town where everyone hates her. It's honestly kind of fun in a way." She arched an eyebrow under her mass of blond curls.

Justine felt her lips curve as she studied the woman who seemed self-assured and lost, both at once. "I'm a divorced attempted murderess, so I don't really have any room to judge."

"Oh, right. Saw that on the news. You should've gone for the jugular. Any man who hits a woman deserves to drown in his own blood." Straightening, she rubbed her chin. "Was that too much? I'm overly dramatic. I'd say I might change, but I'm forty-three, so I think it's probably too late."

Justine grinned and realized she was rapidly growing fond of Heather Combs. Her dry wit and self-deprecating sense of humor was rather charming if you didn't mind the underlying bitchiness. Before she could respond, someone called her name, and she glanced over to see her new neighbor strolling toward them.

"Speaking of dramatic, meet Ardor Creek's newest celebrity and my new neighbor, J.R. Kramer."

"Just Jeremy is fine," he said, extending his hand toward Heather. "Nice to meet you."

"Hello, just Jeremy," Heather said, her tone sultry as she shook his hand. "It's *very* nice to meet you."

Jeremy's eyebrows lifted at her obvious interest. "Uh, thanks. Hi, Justine."

"Hey," she said, cupping his arm. "Thanks so much for coming. Let me show you around."

"Don't be a stranger," Heather called, wiggling her fingers in a wave as Justine led him away.

"Is she a friend of yours?"

"Um, well...not really, but I think there's potential," Justine said. "She has a history in Ardor Creek. I'll tell you all the details one day. For now, let me show you the goods."

She began the tour around the small gallery as the conversation with Heather lingered in her mind. Considering Justine's curious—and nosy—nature, she was excited to uncover more about the woman who'd recently returned to Ardor Creek.

Gary arrived at the showing late due to an incident near the old warehouse on the outskirts of town. The station had received several calls of teenagers drinking and smoking, and he and one of his fellow patrol officers broke it up before he could go home and change. Wanting to look nice for Justine, he wore dress pants, a collared shirt, and a blazer. When he finally arrived at the gallery, he noticed Brenda and Joseph exiting with Avery.

"Hey, Gary," Avery called, running toward him and opening her arms. Feeling his heart swell, he scooped her up and rested her on his hip.

"Hey there. Did you have fun at your mom's showing?"

She nodded. "I'm going to sleep over at Grandma and Grandpa's tonight. Don't tell Mom, but Grandma said I could have one scoop of ice cream before bed!"

His mouth fell open. "One whole scoop? Lucky you. That's pretty awesome, Grandma."

"It's our secret," Brenda said, lifting her eyebrows as she looked at Avery. "Right, dear?"

"Yep."

"Good girl," Brenda said, rubbing her arm as love shined in her gaze.

"Well, I'll let you all get to it. Nice to see you both."

"Good to see you too, Gary," Joseph said. "Justine always tells us how you check on them since you live close by. We appreciate you looking out for our girls."

"It's nothing, sir," he said, handing Avery over to Brenda. "They're two of my favorite people in the whole world."

"You're my favorite," Avery said shyly as she chewed her finger.

"Well, that means a whole lot, Avery. Thank you."

"Say goodnight to Gary, dear."

"Good night."

"Good night, guys. Be safe, okay?"

He gave them one last wave before heading into the gallery and searching for Justine. She was in the corner by one of her sculptures, holding a champagne flute while in deep conversation with a man he'd never met. Was he someone new in town? Perhaps her new neighbor?

Gary sized him up as he reached for one of the flutes on the nearby counter. The guy was tall and good-looking, which unsettled something deep within. Justine had mentioned her new neighbor was divorced, and Gary wasn't quite sure how he felt about that. Suddenly, he found himself wishing that a nice old lady had moved next to Justine so he wouldn't have to see her talk to someone eligible and handsome.

It was a ridiculous thought, but Gary felt it all the same. He always knew the time would come when Justine would meet someone, and he thought he'd be prepared. Unfortunately, his heart had other ideas, and it shattered in his chest as he observed them. The man leaned down to whisper something in her ear, causing her to laugh before she placed her hand on his chest. He wore a suit that was much nicer than Gary's blazer and dress pants ensemble, and he suddenly felt uncomfortable.

Justine must've felt his gaze because she turned to face him and called his name. "Come over. I want to introduce you to Jeremy."

Clutching the glass, he trailed over, offering his hand. "Gary Lincoln."

"Jeremy Kramer. Nice to meet you. Justine mentioned you're one of Ardor Creek's finest."

"He's the finest, hands down," she said, beaming. "Gary is amazing and one of my dearest friends."

Friends. Right. It was all they could ever be. Although it was inherently true, he found himself wanting to smash Jeremy's face in since he'd had the gall to whisper in Justine's ear. Of course, that was absurd—especially because he seemed like a nice guy—so Gary just smiled and sipped his champagne.

"Jus is a gem. You're lucky to be her neighbor. If you'll excuse me, I'm going to browse. Have fun."

"Uh...okay," Justine said, appearing confused. "Let me know if you see anything you like. You can obviously have it for free."

"Of course I'll pay you if I see something that catches my eye," he said, giving an absent salute. Gary didn't know the first thing about fine art, but little bugs of anxiety were now crawling in his stomach after seeing Justine with her neighbor. He spent several minutes perusing the gallery before finishing his champagne and deciding he should head home. It had been a long day, and his rapidly souring mood wasn't doing anyone any favors.

"I'm going to go," he said, approaching Justine as she stood in the back of the gallery talking to Kristoff and Jeremy. "I have a ton of errands to do tomorrow."

"I thought you were off tomorrow. Avery and I might have been secretly planning to bring you freshly made brownies."

"I am, but there's still so much to do." Leaning down, he gave her a quick peck on the cheek. "Your art is gorgeous, Jus. Hope you sell it all. See you later."

Something flashed in her eyes as she gazed at him. "Thanks for coming. See you later."

Sparing a nod, he all but fled from the gallery, silently acknowledging he'd acted like an ass. Sighing, he climbed into his car and drove home, anxious to rip off the uncomfortable clothes and erase the image of Justine laughing with another man from his mind.

Chapter 8

Justine was exhausted by the time the showcase was over. She'd had an excellent night with a rather large haul, and Kristoff was excited as he locked the back door of the gallery.

"You're a star, my dear," he said, jingling the keys in his hand. "Ardor Creek's Picasso, if I do say so myself."

"I'm not sure that's a compliment since I'm the first artist I know of from Ardor Creek," she teased, "but I'll take it. On that note, I'm heading home to take off these heels and put on my slippers."

"You deserve it, Justine. I'll call you next week to plan our next show in the city."

"Sounds great. Thanks for everything."

Strolling to her car, she relaxed behind the wheel and inhaled a calming breath. It had been a wonderful night, and she'd enjoyed talking to Jeremy, Heather, and her parents when they'd stopped by with Avery. Carrie, Peter, Scott, Ashlyn, Mark, Teresa, Chad, and Abby had also made appearances, which warmed her heart. And of course, Gary had shown up as she knew he would.

Biting her lip, she remembered his somewhat terse expression. It elicited an uneasy feeling in her core, and she wondered if he was upset with her for some reason. Had she done something to make him angry? Searching her brain, she couldn't fathom why he would be terse with her. As the feeling bubbled inside, she decided there was only one way to find out. Starting the car, she pulled onto Main Street and set off toward Gary's house.

She arrived a few minutes later, trepidation welling as she exited the car. It was after eleven o'clock, but the notion of seeing Gary was now firmly entrenched in her mind. If there was one thing Justine knew about herself, it was that once she'd set her mind on something, it was going to happen.

Climbing up the porch stairs, she knocked before clutching her cardigan around her shoulders to ward off the breeze. Sounds shuffled behind the door before Gary pulled it open. Justine's eyes drifted over his bare feet, sweatpants, and t-shirt before locking onto his.

"Hi," she said softly.

"Come in." He stepped back, closing the door behind her. "It's chilly tonight."

"That it is," she said, rubbing her arms. "Can we, uh, talk in your living room?"

"Sure." Gesturing with his head, he led her toward the room, turning on the lamp as he directed her toward the couch. "Are you okay, Jus? It's late."

Sighing, she sat on the couch as he sat beside her. "You're always asking me if I'm okay. I allowed that dynamic to happen in our relationship, and I hate it."

"What dynamic?"

"The one where you're the protective cop and I'm the victim." Frustrated, she ran her fingers through her hair. "It's just so...cliché."

"I don't see you as a victim."

Inching closer to him, she gently placed her hand on his shoulder. "I feel like you were annoyed with me tonight and can't figure out why. Did I do something to upset you?"

"I'm not annoyed with you."

Laughing, she shook her head. "You seem annoyed right now. I mean, I did show up at your house unannounced close to midnight. You were probably sleeping."

"I was awake."

"Okaaaaay," she said, craning her neck and moving closer. "Then, why are you acting weird?"

Expelling a breath, he ran a hand over his face. "What do you want me to say here, Jus?"

"I want you to tell me the truth. I'm so tired of this dance we keep starting but refuse to finish. If you don't want to be with me because I fucked up so badly with Dean, just tell me. Or if it's because you don't want to ruin our friendship, I'll accept that too. Tell me so I can digest it and begin to move on, because I'm stuck in this limbo of wanting someone who obviously doesn't want me back."

Resting his fingers on his forehead, he shook his head. "That's ridiculous. Of course I want you."

"You do?" Straightening, she processed his statement. "Because you hold yourself back from crossing that line, and I thought maybe it was because of my history with Dean—"

"It's not," he interrupted, standing and beginning to pace. "It has nothing to do with you."

"Then what is it?" Rising, she approached him, cupping his arms to halt his pacing. "Because sometimes you look at me and I swear you want me too. And then you just...shut it down," she said, circling her hand. "Why?"

"I can't be with you that way, Justine. It's not possible for me."

"Romantically?" she asked, confused.

"Yes," he said tersely.

"Because you're not attracted to me?"

Sighing, he tenderly placed his palms on her cheeks, and she felt them burn under his warm skin. "I'm so attracted to you, Jus."

"Then, I don't understand—"

"I was shot in the thigh," he said, his gaze almost angry as he cupped her face. "Near my pelvic region. Do you understand what that means?"

Comprehension began to dawn as the words settled in. "It affected your ability to, um...perform?"

"Yes," he gritted. Dropping his hands, he turned away, harshly rubbing his eyes. "God, this is so fucking embarrassing. I didn't want to have this discussion with you."

"Why?" Encircling his arm, she gently turned him toward her. "I would never judge you. You can't help something that happened when you were shot, for god's sake. You have no control over that."

"It's easy to say when you haven't experienced it. It ruined my marriage, and I won't let it ruin another relationship that's extremely important to me. I'd rather remain friends, even if it means I have to see you with someone else."

A frustrated huff escaped her lips. "Thanks for deciding my future life choices, but I'm pretty sure I can pick my own partner, thank you very much."

He arched a brow, causing her to bristle.

"Don't throw Dean in my face," she said, pointing at him. "I learned my lesson even if it took me half my life to learn it. I won't make those mistakes again. Next time I choose to be with someone, it will be because I care for him and have the right foundation." Stepping closer, she brushed her body against his. "A foundation like the one we have, Gary."

"No," he said, easing away. "I won't set you up for something I know will fail. You need to go home."

Gripping his arms, she pulled him toward her. "Since when do you have the only say in this? There are two people in this relationship, Gary."

"Because I know how disastrous it will be if we cross the line. I refuse to let it happen."

Eyes narrowing, she stepped back and tugged her cardigan from her shoulders. Tossing it toward the couch, she stood tall and lifted her chin.

"Did you get shot in the face too?"

His features contorted in confusion. "No."

"Good," she said, stepping forward and cupping his jaw. "Because we're about to put those sexy-as-hell lips to good use."

"Jus—"

Lifting to her toes, she drew his face to hers. "Kiss me, Gary."

Warm breaths rushed across her lips as he panted above her. "I can't—"

Lifting a final inch, she cut off the words by cementing her lips to his.

Gary considered himself a strong person, one who stuck by his decisions after carefully weighing the consequences. He'd told himself a million times he would never kiss Justine—never touch her—because it would lead down a road that would end in heartbreak. But the moment she pressed her lips to his, his resolve shattered into a thousand pieces.

Sliding his arms around her waist, he drew her close, moaning into the wet depths of her mouth as he surged his tongue inside. Her high-pitched mewl set his body on fire, and he drew her close, aching to feel her curves against his hardness. Pulling her into his body, he slid his tongue over hers, tasting her before sucking her wet tongue between his lips. She groaned, causing him to shudder as he finally held her in the way he'd always imagined.

Needing more, he cupped the firm globes of her ass, lifting her as she gave a tiny yelp. Her legs instinctively wrapped around his waist, and he carried her to the spot beside the fireplace, resting her back against the wall so he could push his body further into hers. Thrusting his fingers in her short hair, he tugged, tilting her head so he could devour her once again.

Their tongues battled, sluicing over each other as she moaned beneath him. Shock pervaded his veins when he felt himself harden against her mound, and he pressed against her, undulating his hips as she kissed him with ardor. Unable to stop himself, he lowered his hand to her silken thigh, running it over the smooth skin until his fingers brushed her lacy panties.

Breaking the kiss, he stared into her glazed eyes, struggling to breathe as he admired her swollen lips and flushed cheeks. "I swore I wouldn't touch you this way," he whispered, running his finger over the edge of her underwear. "But how am I supposed to stop when you look at me like that, Jus? You're so fucking gorgeous."

"Please," she whispered, spearing her nails into the skin of his nape, driving him wild. "I want to be touched by someone who won't hurt me. It's been so long."

Resting his forehead against hers, he glided his finger under her panties, hissing when he found her wet folds. "I would never hurt you, Jus."

"I know." She pushed against his hand. "I trust you."

The words set something free deep within. Delving between her drenched folds, he found her opening and began to circle as she writhed against him. Lowering his lips to hers, Gary thrust his tongue into her mouth as he surged his finger in her tight channel. Her body shuddered, opening to him as he plundered her mouth and core. Determined to make her scream, he added another finger, searching as he drew her bottom lip between his teeth.

"Fuck!" she cried, undulating against his hand. "I need more..."

"I've got you, hon," he murmured against her lips, nibbling them as he gathered her honey on his fingers. Trailing them up her wet slit, he searched for her clit. Locating the tiny nub, he began to stimulate it with his fingers.

"Oh, right there..." she cried, biting his lip and dragging it into her mouth.

"I'll rub you all night until you come, Jus," he rasped, gently biting her back before drawing her lip into his mouth to suck away the sting. Sucking her lip, he stared into her half-lidded eyes as his fingers continued the steady rhythm.

Her fingers threaded through his hair, tugging him close as she drew him into another blazing kiss. She held nothing back, and he reveled in her openness. Justine put on a brave face, but he understood how hard it must be to open herself to someone after her experience with Dean. The knowledge that he was the man lucky enough to hold her...to touch her...meant more to him than she would ever know.

"I'm so close," she moaned into his mouth. "Oh, *god*...Gary..."

"I'll never let you fall, hon," he murmured, nibbling her lips before swiping his tongue over them. Her eyes rolled back in her head at the sexy action, and she began to tremble violently in his arms.

"Oh...yes! It's...*ohmygod*..."

Suddenly, she exploded in his arms, her frame wracking with shudders as she came. The soft cry of his name on her lips was sweeter than the finest chocolate, and he held her tight, determined to ensure she felt pleasure. Warm laughter surrounded them as she melted against him, pliant and trusting, cementing something deep within. Her trust was such a magnificent gift, and one he would never squander.

Her giggles eventually faded to sated sighs before she lifted her lids and stared deep into his eyes. "Um, hi. You gave me an entire speech about not touching me when you kiss like that? Not cool."

Breathing a laugh, he nudged her nose with his. "I guess I'm okay at it?"

"Way better than okay, buddy. Good grief. And your hands aren't bad either." Biting her lip, she grinned as she tightened her arms around his neck. "That felt so good. I want to return the favor."

Inhaling a deep breath, he shook his head. "I'm not ready, hon. I just..." Struggling to find the words, he shrugged. "I have no idea what will happen if we try. I'm terrified of letting you down."

Running her fingers over his cheek, she studied him. Gary could see the wheels churning in her mind as she contemplated the next move now that they'd crossed an important line.

"I have a proposition."

"Okay," he said, feeling the corner of his lips curve.

"Why don't you come over one night this week? I'll have Avery stay with my parents or with Mark and Teresa. That way, we'll be prepared and can really discuss this like two adults who honor and care for each other." Her fingers were soothing as they stroked the back of his neck. "I understand how hard this must be for you. It's definitely an uncomfortable topic. Embarrassing, even. But I promise I'll listen with an open mind. I don't want to dismiss what's between us if we can figure it out. I care about you, Gary. I want to make love to you. Whatever that looks like and in whatever form we can."

His eyes roved over her flushed features. "I want that too, hon. I just don't want to disappoint you."

"Keep touching me and kissing me like that, and I'll be the happiest woman on the damn planet."

Chuckling, he placed a sweet peck on her lips. "I love touching you. I'd do it every fucking day if I could."

"You *can*," she said, giving him a cheeky grin. "Come over this week and let's talk. Please, Gary."

Sighing, he nodded. "Okay. I'm willing to discuss it with you. It's so embarrassing for me, Jus, but I'll do it."

"Good. Remember, no judgement. Just a nice sex talk between adults."

Laughing, he drew his hand across the silken skin of her thigh before setting her on her feet. "All right."

Running her hands over her dress, she beamed. "I'm so glad I wore a dress tonight. Perfect for you to sneak those sexy hands under." Waggling her eyebrows, she strode to the couch and shrugged on her cardigan. "Well, I guess I'll finally let you go to sleep. Sorry for barging in."

He walked her to the door and stood in the frame as she pivoted atop the porch rug. Lifting to her toes, she gave him one final kiss, and he was thankful he'd have the taste of her on his lips as he fell asleep.

"Dream of me," she said, her tone almost shy as she grinned under the stars.

"I always do, hon." He tucked a tuft of hair behind her ear.

"Night." With a final wave, she trailed down the stairs and entered her car, the headlights illuminating the darkness before she drove away. After a moment, he grabbed his keys and headed to his car, needing to ensure she'd gotten home safely. Her silhouette glowed in the upstairs bedroom window, and he reveled in the fact he'd finally gotten to touch her.

Returning home, he decided not to brush his teeth again since he'd already brushed them when he got home from the gallery. Sliding between the sheets, he rubbed his finger over his lips, treasuring the traces of Justine's lipstick and the remnants of her essence on his skin.

Chapter 9

♥

Justine woke up on Saturday morning with the excitement of a teenager after her first kiss. Squealing, she tugged the covers over her head and kicked her feet atop the bed.

"Finally!" she yelled, laughing as she remembered last night's sexy shenanigans. Who knew that Officer Lincoln had such talented lips and hands? Holy hotness. Now that they'd crossed the line to physical intimacy, she wanted so much more.

Lowering the covers, she gnawed her lip as she stared at the ceiling. She couldn't imagine how embarrassing it must've been for him to tell her he had performance issues. After all this time, *that* had been the reason he'd held himself back. Shaking her head on the pillow, she sighed.

"I don't give a damn about that," she murmured to herself. "You have to figure this out, Justine."

Realizing Teresa was the perfect person to talk to about the irregular situation, she decided she'd pull her aside at Sunday dinner and formulate a plan to ensure she proceeded in a manner that made Gary feel comfortable. Closing her eyes, she imagined him holding her as they were both naked...and trailing those lips over every inch of her body. She had a feeling he would be an unselfish lover who would cherish her and ensure she found pleasure. God, what would that even feel like? Pleasurable sex had been nonexistent during her last few years with Dean.

Giving a tiny squeal, she rose and prepped for the day so she could pick up Avery. They had a nice lazy Saturday together where they watched movies and made brownies, and Justine figured it was the perfect time to feel her out. It wasn't as if Justine needed Avery's permission to date Gary, but she was the most important person to her on the planet, and Justine felt an urge to confirm her daughter would be okay with bringing someone else into the close twosome they'd formed.

"Can we take some to Gary?" Avery asked as she slathered chocolate icing over the warm brownies in the tray.

"We can. You like Gary a lot, huh?"

Avery nodded as she slid the icing with the spatula, her tongue situated between her teeth as she concentrated. "He's nice. You should marry him like Uncle Mark married Teresa."

Laughing, Justine picked up a spatula and began to help her spread the icing. "I don't think we're there yet, but I do want to make sure you're okay with me asking him over more often. You and I have a pretty awesome thing going, and I don't want to mess it up."

"I don't miss Dad, Mom," she said, her blue eyes so genuine. "He was mean. I like Gary a lot better. You can invite him over anytime and maybe he can play in the tree house with me."

"Maybe so," she said, grinning at how sweet she was. "I like him too. You know, if you ever want to talk to me about your dad or have any questions, you can always ask me."

"I know. Teresa told me I can talk to you or her if I ever feel sad."

"That's right, baby." Teresa had done some one-on-one therapy sessions with Avery after Justine's arrest and had assured her Avery was resilient and adjusting well. Still, Justine worried, and her daughter's well-being was her number one priority. "Anytime you need us."

Smiling, she stuck her finger in her mouth and licked off the icing. "Ready! Can we take them to Gary now?"

"Sure. Let me call him and make sure he's home."

Lifting her phone, she dialed his number and held it to her ear, smiling like a dope the entire time it rang.

"Hey," he said in his deep baritone.

"Hey. Avery and I made brownies, but I didn't want to bring them over if you've got a hot date or something."

Chuckling, he said, "Nope. Just watching whatever Marvel movie is on TV while I do laundry."

"Fun. We'll be over in a few then. Do you need me to get milk? If so, I'll drive."

"Nope, I've got a full carton ready to be spilled."

Laughing, she nodded. "Okay. Can't wait to see you. I'm going to talk to Teresa tomorrow about keeping Avery one night this week."

"Okay, hon. Sounds good."

"Bye." Clicking off the phone, she bit her lip as she held it to her chest.

Avery covered her mouth with her fists and began to snicker.

"What are you laughing at, young lady?" she asked, reaching over and tickling her.

Squeals of laughter sounded before she said, "You like Gary."

Resting her head on her fist, she leaned her elbow on the island. "I really like him, baby."

"Yay!" Avery chanted before sliding off her stool and beginning to jump on the tile floor.

"Man, we need to burn off this energy. Keep jumping and maybe we'll jog to Gary's. What do you say?"

Her daughter nodded in agreement, and Justine packed up the brownies as she anticipated seeing the man who'd consumed her thoughts all day.

On Sunday, Justine and Avery had dinner at Mark and Teresa's house. Her brother was an amazing cook and whipped up a paella that was out of this world. Once they finished, Justine asked Teresa if she could speak to her privately on the back porch. After pouring a glass of wine, they headed outside into the brisk fall evening.

"Wow," Justine said, falling into one of the broad-backed seats. "Mark definitely inherited my mom's cooking skills. Dean always said I was a terrible cook. As much as I hate to admit he was right, I'm only really proficient at brownies, mac and cheese, and anything I can toss in the microwave." Rubbing her stomach, she sighed. "I'm stuffed."

"Mark's cooking skills were one of the things I found so attractive about him in the beginning," Teresa said, sipping her red wine. "I can barely cook toast, and he made all this wonderful food when we were fake engaged."

"Um, yeah. I'm pretty sure it was never fake with you guys, but whatever." Sipping her wine, she noticed Teresa's soft grin.

"It probably wasn't. I think we were both just too stubborn to admit it for a while." Turning her head on the seat, she said, "I'm so happy, Justine. I thought the ship had sailed on finding a husband and having a child. It's a good reminder we can't see all the paths our lives will take."

"Is this supposed to be a subtle reminder for me?" She arched a brow.

Chuckling, Teresa shrugged. "Maybe. I know it's hard to love after what you experienced with Dean. I hope you're willing to try again. Maybe our situation can inspire you."

"Well, you must be psychic because that's what I wanted to talk to you about."

She leaned closer. "Do tell."

"Okay, you have to keep this between us. Well, you'll probably tell Mark, and I guess I'm okay with that, but I don't want my parents knowing. I love them but my mom will have me married before the week is over."

Snickering, Teresa nodded. "Okay. You have my word."

Blowing out a breath, she relaxed in the seat. "I finally made a move on Gary."

"Oh, that's fantastic, Justine! How did it go?"

"Good." Lifting her glass, she took a sip of wine. "Really good. My god, Teresa, the man can kiss. I've pretty much fangirled over his lips for the past twenty-four hours."

Teresa's chuckle washed over them. "Good for you. So, he didn't reject you. See? You were worried for nothing."

"Right. So...um, that's kind of what I want to talk to you about. It turns out he was pushing me away because of an issue he has, not because of my history with Dean or because he was worried about ruining our friendship."

"What issue?"

Pursing her lips, she traced her finger over the rim of the wineglass. "He was shot in the line of duty years ago—in his thigh, near the pelvic region."

"Oh. I think I see."

"Yeah. He says it affected his ability to perform...you know, sexually...and that it ruined his marriage."

Teresa's gaze turned contemplative. "That can be devastating to any relationship. I'm so sorry he experienced that."

"Me too. He said he never wanted to touch me because he didn't want to disappoint me, but I honestly don't care, Teresa." Lifting a shoulder, she said, "I mean, penetration doesn't even do it for me, if you know what I mean. I need the stimulation elsewhere."

"I understand." Narrowing her eyes, she pondered. "I've had several clients in couples therapy who experienced performance issues from the male partner. It's easy to say you don't care when you haven't been in the situation."

"That's what he said," she murmured. "I mean, of course, I'd love to connect with him that way...to have him inside me..." Grinning, she asked, "Is this too weird a discussion to have with my sister-in-law?"

"No way," she said, waving her hand. "I'm a therapist and your friend. Let it all out."

Laughing, she nodded. "Okay. Since you have experience with this, I'd love any advice about what to say to him. I'm going to have him over one day this week so we can talk. I asked, and he said he would even though I know it's an embarrassing topic for him. Oh," she said, lifting a finger, "and I'll need you and Mark to take Avery that night, if you don't mind. I could ask Mom, but, you know, meddling."

"We'd be happy to. I'll discuss with him and pick the best night." Settling back in her chair, she considered. "The most important thing is to be honest. You two are already friends, so that one should be pretty easy. You'll also need to figure out the protection situation. It will most likely be easier for him if he doesn't have to wear a condom, but you also need to be safe."

"Got it. Go on. This is good stuff." She waggled her brows.

"In my opinion, the hardest moments will come when you're actually intimate. If he isn't able to perform, or if he begins to perform and loses the ability, you need to remember to be supportive. Many women make it about themselves, but that's rarely the case. A lot of these situations are more mental than physical. If he loses the ability to perform, he'll most likely be embarrassed. It's important that you reassure but don't placate. Just remind him there are other ways to experience intimacy and go back to kissing and embracing. Does that make sense?"

Justine nodded. "Totally. When you see this in your practice, does it get better for the couples over time?"

"It usually does with the ones who follow the directives I mentioned. Communication and acceptance are key. Once either of those is lost, it's a lot harder to reform the bond."

"Got it. Well, I feel really comfortable with Gary and think I can do that. I mean, I haven't been with anyone but Dean, and it's hard for me too, Teresa. Opening myself up that way again..." Swirling the wine, she pushed away the terrible memories that struggled to surface. "If I'm going to do it with anyone, Gary is the one."

"That's so lovely. He's a really wonderful man, Justine."

"He is." Sighing, she looked at the moon, slowly rising as it peeked behind the horizon. "We took him brownies yesterday, and the way he is with Avery..." Biting her lip, she gave a tiny shiver. "Is it weird to be attracted to someone because they're amazing with your daughter? Because it's so hot to me."

"Not weird at all," Teresa said, shaking her head. "It actually affirms how right it could be between you two. I'm so glad you're exploring it."

Inhaling, she straightened and finished the last of her wine. "Me too. I'm going to do my best to be understanding so we can have awesome sexy times. I think we can figure it out."

"I have no doubt. I'm always here if you want to talk."

"Nothing like free therapy. Between me and Avery, I think we owe you a fortune."

Standing, Teresa extended her hand. "That's what family is for, Justine. I'm so happy to be part of your family."

Rising, Justine clenched her hand. "Me too, Teresa. I don't know how you put up with my brother, but I'm really glad you stomach it," she teased.

Laughing, they trailed inside to rejoin the rest of their family.

Chapter 10

On Wednesday, Gary returned home from his shift around six o'clock and headed to his bedroom to change. Justine had informed him that Avery was staying with Mark and Teresa for the night and she would pick her up on Thursday morning to take her to school. Nerves flitted in his belly as he changed into jeans, a black polo shirt, and sneakers. If he was honest, he felt like a damn teenage virgin getting ready for prom. Although he wanted nothing more than to make love to Justine, he knew the chances of them having mind-blowing sex were slim. Knowing that, what the hell was he supposed to do when she looked at him with those pretty eyes and asked him to make love to her? Hell, he no idea. Saying no to Justine was a futile endeavor, and he knew it.

Sighing, he slung on his jacket and began the trek to her house. The crisp fall air flooded his nostrils, and it calmed him slightly as he trod across the grass. He would do his best to be honest with Justine and tell her how disastrous his injury was for his marriage. If she still wanted to try after that...well, he figured she'd just have to kiss him with those sexy lips, and his hesitation would turn to dust.

When he reached her house, he knocked and fiddled with his jacket as her footsteps sounded behind the door. Pulling it open, she gave him a smile that damn near buckled his knees and gestured him inside.

"I made a ton of appetizers for us," she said, leading him into the kitchen. "Figured you'd be hungry after work, and I'm always starving."

Gary noticed the spread of charcuterie, meatballs, bruschetta and some fried doughy things that looked like empanadas. "Thanks, Jus. You didn't have to do this."

"Well, I figured you might not have eaten since you're probably nervous." Pouring them both a glass of red wine, she handed it to him. "Hell, *I'm* nervous. This is a big step for me too."

Clinking his glass with hers, he smiled before taking a sip. "We're a sad bunch, huh?"

Laughing, she sat atop the island stool, and he slid onto the seat beside her. "Seriously," she said, popping a piece of cheese into her mouth. "The injured cop and the attempted murderess. It has a catchy ring to it though." Shrugging, she grabbed a piece of pepperoni and grinned as she chewed.

"Like a bad soap opera," he muttered. Picking up one of the plates, he scooped some meatballs and an empanada onto it before grabbing a fork and digging in. "Mmm...these are good. Thank you."

"Sure thing. I was just telling Teresa the other day I'm not a great cook, but I can usually handle appetizers. Let's get tipsy and full before we tackle the big stuff, okay?" Lifting her glass, she took a sip before loading her own plate with food. "How was your day?"

They fell into conversation, and he told her about the dispute he'd handled between two neighbors who couldn't agree on how tall the bushes should be between their houses. Justine told him about the vase she was making for her mom as a surprise birthday present. The conversation was easy, as it had always been between them, and Gary realized if he was ever going to attempt to have sex again, he was happy it was with her.

"What are you grinning about?" she asked.

Sliding his hand over hers, he squeezed. "I just like hanging with you, Jus."

Turning her hand, she laced their fingers. "I like it too. You're such a good man. I wish I'd met you before Dean. Well, I guess I technically did, but you were older. Mark's friends thought his little sister was too dorky to hang out with. And then I got married so young. Man, I was daft."

"I got married young too. I've always been a commitment kind of guy. Nicole and I lost our virginities to each other, and I loved her, so the next step was marriage. I never really had the urge to play the field."

"Dean is the only person I've been with. Ugh." She rolled her eyes. "I'm excited to actually try with someone new. It certainly wasn't great once he started hurting me."

"I'm so sorry he hurt you." He smoothed his thumb over the soft skin of her hand. "Sometimes, I wish I'd beaten the shit out of him. Probably would've lost my job, but it might have stopped him."

"Nothing can stop an abuser when they're determined," she said, shaking her head. "Took me a long time to learn that. And I finally learned to protect myself, which is the lesson I needed. You couldn't have saved me. I had to save myself."

"And look at you now." Resting his chin on his fist, he gazed at her. "You're so strong, Jus. I'm so proud of you. I hope that doesn't sound weird or deprecating. It's just the truth."

"I'm pretty damn proud of myself," she said, patting herself on the shoulder.

Their chuckles mingled as they finished the appetizers, and she stood, wiping her hands on her napkin. "Okay, I'm thinking we can talk in the living room. Sound good?"

"Sure." Standing, he followed her down the hallway, heart pounding the entire time. They sat on the plushy couch, and she tucked one leg underneath as she smiled. "So, let's start with the fact you rocked my world on Friday. It was awesome, and there's no way in hell I'm letting you off the hook without touching me again."

Resting his arm on the back of the couch, he grinned. "I'm glad. I've dreamed of touching you like that for a long time, hon."

Tilting her head, she asked, "Why did you never tell me?"

Pursing his lips, he glanced at the ceiling before reclaiming her gaze. "My sexual issues ended my marriage, Jus. It's not something I wanted to saddle you with."

"From what I remember, you and Nicole had issues before you were shot."

"That's true. The one thing that always brought us back was our sexual connection, and then I lost the ability to do that. It was the nail in the coffin."

Her eyes darted over his face. "I know this is embarrassing, but I'm curious. You were shot in a major vessel, I'm guessing?"

"Yes," he said, swiping his hand over his face. "It inhibits my ability to get an erection, or if I do get one, sometimes I can't maintain it." Sighing, he shook his head. "It's something I can't control, and when you're in the heat of the moment, it's so damn infuriating."

Gnawing her lip, she pondered. "Well, I'll tell you that I don't climax from penetration. I need to be stimulated on the spot you found on Friday." She waggled her brows. "So, penetration isn't the hugest deal for me, although I do like the intimacy it creates."

"I'd love nothing more than to connect with you that way, hon. I just don't know how I'll perform, and I don't want to let you down."

"Well, let's set some ground rules. It's probably easier for you if you don't have to wear a condom, right?"

"Yes," he said with a nod. "The stronger the sensation, the easier it is for me."

"Okay. I haven't been with anyone since Dean and am tested every year at my gynecology visits. I'm clean and will be happy to show you the results."

"Same here, and I haven't been with anyone since Nicole."

"I went back on the pill after I had Avery, so we're good there." Scooting closer, she slid her hand over his thigh. "Now, let's talk about this notion you'll disappoint me." Her lips formed a sultry smile. "Were you in the same room with me on Friday? You made me feel so damn good, Gary."

Breathing a laugh, he edged closer, palming her cheek. "I'm glad, but you might not feel the same when we're in the heat of the moment."

"Well," she said, shrugging, "we won't know unless we give it a shot." Standing, she extended her hand. "I propose we go for it and see what happens."

Trepidation welled inside as he hesitated.

"I have no expectation except to be held and kissed by you. Everything else is a bonus. Come on."

Swallowing thickly, he slid his hand into hers and followed her up the stairs.

Justine led Gary to her bedroom, determined to ensure they were both comfortable as the night progressed. Drawing him to the center of the room, she toed off her shoes and stood on the plushy carpet as he eyed the queen-size bed.

"Is that the bed you shared with Dean?" he asked, pointing.

"Ew," she said, wrinkling her nose. "No way. I wanted to burn the old one, but it required too much energy. I just had it carted away when I bought this one after our divorce."

Blowing out a breath, he nodded. "Thank god. That would've been really weird."

"Ya think?" Grinning, she pointed at his sneakers. "Take off your shoes and come sit on the bed with me."

Releasing her hand, he bent down and removed his shoes and socks as Justine slid over the comforter. He strode over to sit beside her, and she shimmied into his side.

"Okay, first things first. I'm dying for you to kiss me. Let's start there."

His lips twitched as he turned to face her. Sliding his hands around her waist, he lifted her and straddled her atop his thighs. "Are you always this bossy in the bedroom?"

Encircling his neck, she gave him a sexy smile. "Nope, but you bring it out in me. And I'm also digging the whole thing where you pick me up and maneuver me around." Wiggling into his body, she leaned forward. "There's something primal about it, and I'm here for it."

"I feel pretty primal around you, hon," he murmured, swiping the hair at her temple. "And protective...and possessive. I almost lost it when I saw you talking to Jeremy at the gallery. I wanted to drag you home and never let you go."

"Kinky," she said, nudging his nose with hers. "And now I under-stand why you were so grumpy."

"I told myself I could let someone else have you," he almost whispered, clenching her hair in his fist. "But now that I've touched you, I don't think that's possible."

Sighing against his lips, she burrowed into him. "I don't want anyone else but you."

Breathing her name, he pressed his lips to hers and drew her close. Justine moaned, so thrilled to be in his arms again, and extended her tongue, gliding it over his as his free hand cupped her ass. His tongue plundered her mouth as he held her, his fingers twining in her hair as his strong hand dug into the flesh beneath her tight jeans.

Arousal rushed to her core, and she undulated atop his thighs, wondering if the stimulation was helping. "Is this okay?" she asked, rubbing her jean-clad mound against his zipper.

"Yes," he rasped, capturing her lips in another torrid kiss. "It feels so good, Jus."

Thrilled at the words, she speared her tongue between his lips, finding his tongue and swirling around it. Cool air rushed against her back, and she realized he was bunching her shirt in his hand. Drawing back, she lifted her arms high as he gathered the fabric and tugged the shirt over her head before tossing it to the floor.

His eyes glazed over with lust as he stared at her breasts in her lacy pink bra. Justine was slight and her breasts were small, but he seemed enamored as he cupped them in his hands. His thumbs trailed across the skin that rose above the small cups, back and forth, and she shuddered.

"God, your hands are so hot."

"My hands?" he asked, eyebrows drawing together.

"Yes. Among other things. Keep going." She bit her lip and pushed her breasts into his palms.

Brown eyes simmered as they seared into hers, and Justine felt her entire body flush. Hooking his fingers beneath the cups of her bra, he tugged them down, revealing her nipples. The sensitive buds pebbled under his gaze, and he gently began caressing them with the pads of his thumbs. Desire shot straight to her core, and she felt a surge of moisture between her thighs.

"Don't tease me," she pleaded as he continued the maddening caresses.

"I've waited years to touch you like this, Justine," he murmured in that sexy baritone. "There's no way in hell I'm rushing this."

Sparks of pleasure tingled throughout her frame as he circled his thumbs over the taut nubs. Eventually, he began plucking and tugging the sensitive buds as heavy breaths exited his lungs.

"I swear I'm going to come from you playing with my nipples," she rasped, writhing against him. "It's intense, but it feels amazing."

"I have to taste you," he murmured, cupping one breast and lifting it to his lips. Sliding his mouth over the puckered nipple, he drew her inside, closing his eyes as if he were tasting the finest delicacy. The sensation rocked her body, and she clung to him, needing a guidepost as he loved her so sweetly.

Gary dragged his tongue over her nipple in a slow slide that drove her wild before lightly clamping his teeth on the turgid flesh. Justine groaned as he tugged her nipple, the slight prick of pleasure-pain sending jolts of arousal to her center. At this rate, she was going to soak through her damn jeans she was so aroused.

"I need to take my pants off."

"Not yet," he said, trailing kisses to her other breast. "I need to play with this one too."

Justine groaned at the pleasurable torture as he chuckled against her heated skin. Drawing her other nipple between his lips, he proceeded to lather it with his tongue before tugging it into a hardened point with his teeth.

"The fucking toothpicks," she muttered.

"Huh?" he asked, shooting her a confused look.

"I knew you'd be good at that after I saw you with the toothpicks. Your tongue is all sorts of talented."

Laughing against the curve of her breast, he reached behind and unclasped her bra. "The toothpicks helped me adjust after I ditched my smoking habit. Don't really need them anymore, but I'm glad you were into it." Dragging her bra from her body, he straightened before running his palms over his handiwork. "They're so tight," he murmured, gently squeezing her nipples. "So pretty."

"Okay, we're moving to the 'pants off' portion of the evening. I'm putting my foot down." Shimmying off his thighs, she unzipped her jeans and began to shrug them off. "You too, buddy."

He stood, his expression slightly hesitant, and she encircled his upper arm, forcing him to meet her gaze. "No expectations. Just us. If you want to leave on your underwear, I'm fine with that. Whatever you feel comfortable with."

Nodding, he pulled off his shirt before removing his jeans. Justine slid over the comforter and rested her head on the pillow as she lay on her back. He followed behind, clad only in his boxer briefs, and loomed over her.

"Let me kiss you everywhere and make you come," he said, placing a soft kiss on her lips. "And then, we'll see where I'm at."

Grinning, she slid her arms around his neck. "I'd be a fool to say no to that."

Breathing a laugh, he cemented his lips to hers, kissing her thoroughly before trailing kisses down her neck and over her collarbone then focusing on her breasts again. He licked and sucked her nipples, bringing them back to turgid points before he moved lower. His lips kissed a path over her abdomen, stopping at her navel to dip his tongue inside.

She slid her fingers in his hair, gazing into his gorgeous eyes as he licked her in the intimate spot. Pressing one last kiss to her navel, he slid down farther and situated himself between her legs. Balancing on his knees, he palmed her inner thighs, gently pushing them apart.

Justine opened herself to him, understanding she had to express openness if she expected it in return. Breath shuddered from his lungs as he stared at her deepest place.

"Jesus, honey," he drawled, gently touching two fingers to her core. "You're so wet."

"I'm so into you, Gary," she said, gazing at him from the pillow. "And you kind of went to town on my nipples. It drove me insane."

His lips curved into a sexy smile. "Good. I'm about to do the same to your pussy. If you want to latch onto my hair, you can. I like having it pulled."

Reaching down, she threaded her fingers through his thick brown hair. Giving him a playful grin, she gently drew him to her core.

"You little minx," he teased, letting her steer him to her wet center. "Come here." Lowering his lips to her folds, he began to lick the swollen, wet skin as she clenched his hair.

"Oh my god," she breathed, pushing herself into his skillful mouth as he sucked and nibbled. "Yesssss...*Gary*..."

He growled against her core, the sound sending vibrations of pleasure through her entire body as he pushed deeper. Pressing his fingers against the swollen flesh, he separated her folds, baring her sensitive spots to his lips and tongue. Justine writhed on the bed as he traced the tip of his tongue over her wet skin before trailing it to the engorged bud nestled below the hood. Stretching her with his fingers, he exposed her clit and began flicking it with his tongue.

She purred in ecstasy as he alternated between licking her with that skillful tongue and circling the pads of his fingers over the swollen bud. As her body reached for ultimate pleasure, he closed his mouth over her clit, drawing it between his lips and sucking her deep within.

"Tongue...there...don't stop..." she commanded, legs shaking as they vibrated around his head. Grasping his hair, she pulled him against her, emitting a joyful laugh when he groaned. The actions of his lips and tongue against her clit were frantic, and Justine felt herself begin to tumble over the edge.

"Coming...now...*oh, fuck!*"

Her spine snapped, pushing her pussy deeper into his face as she dove over the cliff toward a blinding orgasm. Gary moaned, the ministrations of his mouth and tongue ardent even though she was shattering into a million pieces. Clenching his hair, she allowed the climax to slam into every part of her frame as she gasped for air. Needing a reprieve, she wrapped her legs around his head, attempting to communicate she couldn't take anymore.

He must've gotten the message because the movements of his mouth ceased. Groaning, she let the shudders claim her as he nestled between her thighs.

Eventually, the flashes behind her eyelids dimmed, and her muscles relaxed on the bed. Slowly lifting her lids, she gazed down to find a sated Gary Lincoln, his cheek resting on her thigh as he grinned.

"Oh, my, Officer Lincoln," she breathed, still struggling to catch her breath. "I... Damn, I'm never speechless. What did you do to me?"

Chuckling, he ran his palm over her leg in a gentle caress. "God, Jus, I could watch you come all day long. You're so beautiful."

Tears burned her eyes as her thoughtful, gorgeous man gazed back at her with tenderness and affection. It was everything she'd ever wanted from her ex-husband, and she wished she hadn't wasted so much time on the wrong man. Reaching for him, she ran her fingers over his jaw. "Somewhere along the way, I convinced myself I didn't need to feel good during sex," she whispered, "or maybe that I didn't deserve to."

His eyebrows drew together before he shifted, slowly climbing over her and aligning their bodies. Stroking the hair at her temple, he stared deep into her eyes. "You deserve everything, Jus. Do you hear me?"

She nodded, overwhelmed by the moment and the blinding orgasm. Unable to control the emotion raging through her body, she felt a single tear fall. He swiped it away before placing a tender kiss on her lips. "No one is ever going to hurt you again. I'll never let that happen."

"I know," she rasped, tracing her fingers over his cheek.

Placing his elbow on the mattress, he rested his head on his palm, gently stroking her collarbone as her skin cooled. They gazed into each other's eyes, communicating without words, and Justine felt her eyes droop.

"Damn it," she muttered before yawning. "It's your turn. I need to wake up."

Something flashed in his eyes before he shook his head. "I don't think he's going to work right now," he said, glancing down at the juncture of his thighs. "Can I just hold you for a while? If you fall asleep, that's fine. We can try round two in a few hours."

"Okay. Maybe I can rub your scalp while we lie here. You seemed to enjoy it when I was digging my nails in there." She gave a tiny snicker.

"I love having my scalp scratched. Go for it."

"Let me pull back the covers."

They shifted around as she maneuvered the bedding. Shuffling underneath the soft fabric, she nuzzled into him when he drew her against his body. Lifting her hand, she threaded her fingers in his hair before beginning to run her nails over his scalp. A sexy groan rumbled in his chest under her ear, and she smiled.

"Feel good?" she mumbled.

"Fuck yes."

Snuggling into him, she threw her leg over his thighs and continued the ministrations until sleep dragged her under its spell.

Chapter 11

Gary awoke to the magnificence of having Justine wrapped around his entire body. She snored softly as her head rested on his chest, and he felt his cock jerk against his stomach. Surprise skated through his frame at his arousal, and he reached down to encircle the flesh, needing confirmation. Sure enough, he was hard as hell and ready to go.

Justine shifted against him and lifted her head, staring at him with sleepy eyes. Realization entered the light-brown orbs, and she slid her hand down to cup his cock. Gary moaned as she began to jerk his shaft above his underwear.

"Take these off," she whispered, tugging at the fabric.

Gary complied, shrugging off the boxer briefs and tossing them to the floor. She rolled onto her back, and he slid over her, telling himself to focus on her gorgeous eyes instead of the anxiety that welled inside. If he began focusing on the fact he might lose the erection, it would most likely happen. Wanting to prepare her, he slid his hand down her body and between her folds.

She murmured a soft moan when he circled her opening, and lust roared within. Was he finally going to make love to her after all this time? The thought brought him immense joy as he glided his fingers to her clit and began stimulating the taut bundle of nerves.

"You can go inside me," she whispered, snaking her fingers through the hair at the back of his neck. "I'm ready."

"You sure?"

She nodded against the pillow, and his heartbeat kicked into overdrive. Gliding over her, he aligned the tip of his cock with her opening, sliding it through the slickness that was rapidly forming. Hissing at the contact, he closed his eyes in ecstasy. Wanting to stare deep into her eyes the first time he slipped inside her, he forced his lids open and began to push.

"*Justine...*" he whispered, advancing inch by slow inch into her tight channel.

"I'm right here," she breathed, cupping his jaw as her other hand clenched his hair.

"If you only knew..." Lowering, he began to gently kiss her as he pushed deeper into her body. Her tight, wet walls choked him in a pleasurable vise until he eventually reached the hilt. Resting his weight on his forearms, he threaded his fingers through her short hair and began to move his hips.

He dragged his cock through her slick folds slowly, wanting to savor every moment. Her sexy whimpers spurred him on as he ached to please her. Lifting his hand, he licked his fingers before sliding them back to her clit, intent on making her come while he was inside her.

"You don't have to do that," she rasped, her hips jutting up to meet his. "It's okay if you focus on your pleasure this time, Gary."

He shook his head, unable to speak as his cock slid back and forth inside her body. His fingers circled her clit, and he hoped they could reach their peaks together. Groaning, he began to move his hips faster, gritting his teeth as he felt a shooting pain in his thigh.

"Fuck," he rasped, feeling his cock begin to soften as the pain took hold. "Damn it. I'm going to lose it."

"Hey," she said, cupping his face and gazing at him with understanding eyes. "That's okay. If it happens, it happens. Keep trying."

He thrust inside her, knowing the effort was futile. Blood surged away from his shaft, and he felt the terrible swell of anger and embarrassment in his chest. Giving a frustrated groan, he slipped from her body and buried his face in her neck.

"Goddammit!"

"Shh..." she soothed, stroking his scalp with her fingernails. "I've got you."

Squeezing his eyes in frustration, he sighed against her skin. "I'm sorry."

"This support thing goes both ways, Gary," she murmured, kissing his temple. "I just want to hold you right now. And I'd love it if you'd hold me back."

Inhaling a deep breath, he slid his arms around her, surprised when his embarrassment began to wane, if only a little. Perhaps because it was Justine and he felt so comfortable with her. Perhaps because she was so understanding and supportive as she held him close. Nicole had always fumed when he wasn't able to perform, and Justine's reaction was a complete one-eighty.

She slid her leg over his, wrapping him against her body as they relaxed. Lifting his head, he gathered the courage to look her in the eye. "Well, that sucked."

Smiling, she shook her head against the pillow. "It was actually really good there for a while. I loved having you inside me that way."

"I loved it too," he said, stroking her cheek. "I'm sorry I lost it."

Compassion entered her gaze as she smoothed the hair at his temple. "Can you do me a favor?"

He nodded.

"It would mean a lot to me if you took the word 'sorry' out of the equation here. I don't want you to apologize if this happens again. Apologizing means you did something wrong or made a mistake, and having a natural reaction to an injury isn't either of those things. Let's just accept this will happen sometimes. When it does, we'll just hold each other afterward." Her lips curved before she bit her lip. "I really like holding you like this, Gary."

He smiled, overcome by her acceptance and graciousness. "Okay. I'll try. Thank you for being so understanding."

"Not that I want to discuss your ex-wife while we're lying here naked, but I'm assuming she wasn't supportive?" She arched an eyebrow.

"Um, no," he muttered, shaking his head. "It was pretty much a disaster every time this happened."

"Well, that sucks. I've had enough of my own disasters, thank you very much. I don't want to recreate them with you. Let's keep this relationship disaster-free. I think we both deserve it."

Chuckling, he pecked her lips. "We definitely do."

"And I already have ideas of things we can try. I have this super-awesome lube I use with my handy-dandy vibrator. It heats up the skin and makes things tingle all over." She waggled her eyebrows. "I think we should use it on you and see where that goes."

"I'm game. I'm willing to try things with you as long as you're okay with the fact they might not work."

"Totally fine with that. I mean, trying is the fun part, right?"

He squinted one eye. "Uh, I'm not convinced, but whatever you say."

Laughing, she ran her fingernails over his jaw where his shadow was beginning to fill in. "We'll get there eventually. One day, we're going to have simultaneous orgasms and then give each other the biggest high-five in history."

Tossing back his head, he gave a raucous laugh. "Damn, that's funny. I can see it in my head."

"Me too." Biting her finger, she said shyly, "I want to use your handcuffs too. I've been having really hot dreams about you using them on me. But, you know, not to arrest me and stuff me in a squad car like last time."

"I hated having to cuff you," he said softly, "but it was policy. I tried my best to help and did everything I could."

"You were so helpful that night and so many other times. You're like my secret protector. It's so sweet."

"I wish I had protected you better." He swiped a tuft of hair away from her forehead. "I should've done more."

"Okay, enough about that night. It's done, and I'm so glad it's behind me. But we're still using the handcuffs, buddy."

Smiling, he nodded. "Okay. That sounds fun."

"Sure does." Lifting her phone from the bedside table, she checked the time. "It's two a.m. and I'm wide awake. Want to go downstairs and finish the apps? I could definitely manage a late-night app and wine session."

"Sure." Leaning down, he placed a soft kiss on her lips. "Thank you, Justine."

"No 'thank yous' or 'I'm sorrys', okay?" she asked, lifting a finger. "When you care about someone, you don't need those words. Got it?"

"Got it." Sliding off her, he reached for his boxer briefs and tugged them on while she slipped on a robe. He reached for his shirt, but she encircled his wrist, stilling his arm.

"No way, Officer Lincoln. This will be a shirtless late-night snack for you. I need to look at that sexy chest."

He rubbed his palm over his pecs. "I try to work out a few times a week to stay in shape for our required annual physicals. It helps ease the pain in my thigh and makes me pretty toned, I guess."

"Toned," she said, shooting him a droll look. "Your body is way hotter than 'toned,' but we'll go with that." Extending her hand, she shook it. "Come on. I'm starving."

Grasping tightly, he followed her from the bedroom.

After finishing another round of appetizers and wine, Justine cleaned up the kitchen and faced her new lover.

"Can you come back upstairs with me and sleep for a bit? I know we both have to be up early."

He rubbed the back of his neck as he contemplated. "I'm fine staying with you, but I have to get up around 5:30 a.m. to head home and shower before work."

"That gives us a few hours to cuddle and sleep," she said, giving him a cheeky grin. "You've already stayed over most of the night. Might as well finish it. I'm sleepy from the wine, so I expect to be able to make out with you for about three point two seconds before I crash again."

Chuckling, he nodded. "Okay, let's do it."

They trailed back upstairs, and she shrugged off her robe, noting he'd left his underwear on before climbing in and pulling her close. She realized he must have scarring around his thigh and might be sensitive about her seeing it. Not wanting to push him, she snuggled into his side and gave him a long, thorough kiss before resting her cheek on his chest and falling into a deep slumber.

The buzzing of his phone woke her up at 5:30 a.m. on the dot, and she groaned as he sat up and clicked it off. "Too early," she mumbled.

Chuckling, he leaned down to kiss her. "Life of a patrol cop. Long hours for extra overtime so you can hopefully buy a house."

Her eyes roved over his broad shoulders and strong legs as he dressed. "You won't buy one too far away, will you? Avery and I like having you close."

Padding to stand beside the bed, he gently smoothed her hair. "I'm an Ardor Creek lifer and like this area of town." Lowering, he whispered in her ear. "And I really like being close to you and Avery, so definitely not too far. Hope you have a good day, hon."

Lifting her lips to his, she gave him a sweet kiss before he turned to walk to the door. Once there, he pivoted and gripped the frame, appearing to ponder his words.

"I loved last night, Jus. Everything about it. Thank you for being...well, for being you, I guess."

Although she'd told him to leave the "thank yous" behind, her lips curved into a warm smile. "You're welcome. Thank you for the orgasms."

"Always," he said in a tone that might have singed her panties off if she were wearing any. "See you later. I'll lock the bottom lock behind me." Tapping the door twice with his fist, he turned and headed down the stairs.

Justine waited until she heard the front door close and the click of the lock before she squealed in delight. After one night with Gary, she was hooked. Never had she felt so cherished as when he gazed at her with those gorgeous eyes as he kissed every inch of her body. And when his strong arms surrounded her as they slept, all hints of loneliness had vanished.

Justine hadn't dated...well, ever, really. She and Dean had just sort of started making out, then banging, and then living together. Before she knew it, she was in a relationship. She had no idea how other women functioned on dating apps, but she had no desire to play that game. Wrinkling her nose, she realized she'd be awful at it.

No, she was a relationship kind of woman, and from what Gary had told her last night, he was a relationship kind of man. Would he be open to them dating exclusively? To becoming each other's partner?

"Simmer down, Justine," she muttered to herself. "Don't scare him away when you just figured out how to lure him in." Giggling at the musings, she shook her head. "One day at a time."

As she showered, the image of his handsome face lingered in her mind. She washed between her legs, noting she was a bit sore. Gary hadn't been inside her for too long, but he'd certainly left his mark. He might have some issues, but when he was hard, he was *big*. Shivering at the thought of getting him fully aroused so he could achieve orgasm, Justine decided she'd stock up on the lube she was so fond of. A little extra wouldn't hurt, right?

Exiting the shower, she dressed and headed over to pick up Avery from Mark and Teresa's. They lived in a nice neighborhood comprised of new houses Scott had built. Carrie and Peter lived next door, and they often had the crew over for cookouts when it was warm. Justine had never attended when she was with Dean—mostly due to the fact she was consumed with being the doting wife at home—but she'd attended quite a few since her divorce. Gary also attended his fair share when he wasn't on duty, and Justine found herself grinning at the thought of showing up to one as his date. Wouldn't that just throw the Ardor Creek rumor mill for a loop?

"Hey, Mom," Avery called, running toward her after she parked in Mark's driveway.

Justine's heart swelled at seeing her baby girl with her arms wide open, beckoning for a hug. Crouching down, she picked her up and swung her around as they giggled.

"Hey, baby. Did you have fun with Aunt Teresa?" Halting the twirl, she kissed her on the nose.

"Yes. Abby brought Kitana over, and I played with her while Teresa and Abby watched Rose and Zoey."

"That sounds fun."

Nodding, she formed a gap-toothed grin. "I want a dog, Mommy."

Justine playfully rolled her eyes. "Oh, now I'm 'Mommy' again? You only call me that anymore when you want something, you little stinker." She tickled Avery's stomach as her daughter squealed with laughter.

"I should've thought about the dog situation," Teresa said, approaching in her robe as the morning sunlight washed over them. "I think that was a mom-foul. I'm sorry."

"It's okay," Justine said, setting Avery on her feet. "I'll consider it..."—she observed Avery's wide, excited eyes—"*if* Avery can show me she can finish her chores every week."

"I can," she said, making an "X" over her heart. "Promise, Mom."

"Okay, we'll see. Go on and get in the car so we can get to school." She jogged toward Justine's car, and Justine enveloped Teresa in a warm embrace. "Your advice rocked. Thank you so much, and thanks for watching Avery."

"You're welcome, and I'm so glad," she said, drawing back and cupping Justine's arms. "Does this mean we'll be seeing more of Gary?"

"God, I hope so." Lifting crossed fingers, she bit her lip. "I'm going to try like hell. I already told myself to calm the fuck down. I don't want to scare him away."

Chuckling, Teresa shook her head. "I don't think that's possible. Mark seems to think he's been in love with you for years, Justine."

Sighing with amused wonder, she ran her hand through her hair. "I had no idea. Am I just an oblivious idiot?"

"You were involved in a terrible marriage," Teresa said, placing her palms on Justine's shoulders. "It's hard to be open to receiving love when you've been hurt. I'm glad you're open to it now."

"I'm so open. Hope he's ready." Lifting her keys, she jiggled them. "Okay, let me get this one to school. Mark will be home from Scranton on Friday, right?"

"Yes. He has a big trial there this week, so he's staying in a hotel until Friday. I miss him so much when he's not here."

"Look at us two lovesick dopes." She rolled her eyes. "Who would've guessed? Have a good day, Teresa." Giving a wave, she trailed to the car, noting how light her step was. One night of intimacy and she was toast. Snickering at the thought, she drove Avery to school and then headed to Main Street. Peter had prepared some financial documents for the LLC she'd recently formed for her artwork, and she figured today was as good as any to stop by and sign them.

"Hey, Justine," Carrie said when she arrived at Peter's office, which he shared with Scott Grillo's contracting company called Grillo Design and Construction, or GDC for short. "How's it going?"

"Good," she said, resting her palms on the high counter as Carrie grinned behind the computer screen. "Peter prepared some forms for me, and I think I have to sign something for him also?"

"Oh, right, he mentioned that to me. There's a form you need to sign since you've officially hired him as your accountant and some other forms for the LLC. Pretty cool you're making enough from your art to start an LLC. I'm so proud of you, Justine."

"Thanks. I had no idea how I'd fare after everything that went down with Dean, but I guess I've done a pretty good job."

"You've done great," she said, her jaw maneuvering as she chewed her gum. "Peter will be here any minute. He drove the kids to school and daycare this morning so I could come in and finish the formatting for some estimates for Scott."

"Cool."

Carrie's eyes narrowed as she assessed her. "You look different. What happened? New haircut?"

"Nope," she said, fluffing her hair. "Same as always. You know I like to dye it different colors. I'm thinking light blue if I ever get around to it, but I haven't found the time."

Squinting one eye, Carrie continued to contemplate before she inhaled a quick gasp. "Justine Lancaster! Did you make a move on Ardor Creek's hottest cop? Oh my god, did you get *laid*?" Leaning forward, she rested her elbows on the desk and placed her chin on her crossed hands. "Tell me everything!"

Justine shook her head in awe. "How could you possibly know that? I swear, you have some sort of radar or something."

Giving a confident smirk, Carrie mimicked brushing dirt off her shoulder. "I'm a pro, honey. I want all the juicy details."

"Which is why I should probably shut the hell up right now."

"No way, sister. You're glowing, so it must've been good."

Sighing, Justine tilted her head. "It was better than good. Amazing, really. I'm a goner, Carrie. I really like him."

"Hot damn," she said, slapping the desk. "It's about time you got some sweet lovin' from a man as awesome as Gary. So, are you guys, like, official? Can I tell people?"

Justine gnawed her lip as she considered. "We haven't really discussed that yet."

"Well, you have his number, right? Call him and ask."

"Are you daft?" she asked, splaying her hands. "I can't call him and ask him if he wants to date me exclusively."

"Why not?"

"Because..." Trailing off, Justine realized she couldn't think of a good reason. "I just... Isn't that weird? Or needy?"

"Not in the least," she said, waving her hand. "Call him now. Tell him I'm dying to know. Come on."

Little bugs of anxiety crawled in her stomach as she contemplated. Deciding she had nothing to lose, she pulled her phone from her pocket and dialed Gary's number. Sure, he might think it strange, but Justine knew he was really into her too. Why not just make it official?

"Hey, hon," he said, and she could tell he was on his Bluetooth in his patrol car from the background noise. "I won't ask if you're okay because you seem to hate it."

She breathed a laugh. "I don't hate it. But I'm calling with a question of sorts."

"Okay. Go for it."

Kicking the short carpet with her shoe, she dredged up the courage to ask him to be her...boyfriend? Were they too old for that? Partner? Hell, she had no idea. "Carrie kind of figured out what happened between us last night."

"She kind of figured it out," he repeated, amusement in his tone.

"Uh, yeah. Anyway, I'm standing here in front of her at GDC and she's asking me if we're dating. So, I figured I'd call you before I say anything since she has the propensity to be a bit chatty around town." She winked at Carrie as the woman wrinkled her nose.

"That's up to you, hon. I'd love nothing more than to be exclusive with you, but I'm not sure that's really fair to you."

"Why?"

"Well...uh..." He cleared his throat. "I mean, you've seen my issues up close. I don't want to burden you with something you're not ready for."

"Man, you are seriously dense sometimes, Gary. I had an amazing time last night. I would love to be your girlfriend. And yes, I know we're probably too old to call each other boyfriend and girlfriend. But I'd like to date you exclusively if you're open to it."

"I'm open."

Silence stretched over the phone as she smiled. "Okaaaaaay. Last chance to renege, because I'm going to tell Carrie once we're off the phone."

His deep chuckle surrounded her as she beamed. "Tell everyone in town for all I care. I'm honored to date you, Jus. You're really special."

"Well, you've done it now. Enjoy your last hour of freedom before the whole town knows."

"Hey!" Carrie called.

Justine scrunched her features at her as Gary laughed. "Okay, hon. I'm heading to a call. Gotta go."

"Be safe. I'll text you later."

Clicking off the phone, she stuck it in her back pocket as Carrie ran from behind the desk. Clutching each other's hands, they began to jump up and down as they squealed. And then, Carrie began the exceedingly fun task of telling everyone in Ardor Creek that Justine Lancaster and Gary Lincoln were officially off the market.

Chapter 12

Gary all but skipped through the week, excited as a kid who'd eaten a thousand bushels of cotton candy. When Justine called to ask if he wanted to be exclusive, his heart had slammed in his chest so hard he thought the damn thing might pop out of his body. But they'd both confirmed they were commitment types, and they'd been friends forever, so if she wanted to take that leap, he'd follow her over the cliff all day long.

Of course, he still had concerns that once the newness of their romantic relationship wore off, she might become frustrated if he couldn't perform. But Gary also understood he couldn't transpose Nicole's reactions on Justine, so he would continue to foster openness and honesty between them. He hoped that if she began to feel annoyed or frustrated, she would tell him so they could try and find a solution.

He worked tirelessly for the rest of the week and mainly communicated through text with Justine. On Friday, she texted him to schedule their weekend plans.

Justine: Hey, lover. Avery and I were hoping you could come hang with us on Sunday since it's your day off.

Gary grinned while he answered her from his patrol car as he sat on the highway on the outskirts of town. The radar gun was on, but it hadn't registered a blip in at least an hour, so hearing from her cured his boredom.

Gary: I'd love to. Don't you go to your family's on Sundays though?

Justine: Usually, but Avery and I wanted a day just for us. We decided to invite you, but that's it. You should feel extremely honored. I might make mac and cheese for you.

Chuckling, his thumbs moved over the keyboard.

Gary: I love mac and cheese. What time should I come over?

Justine: Any time after eleven is fine. We can have lunch and maybe play with Avery outside. It's supposed to be a nice day.

Gary: I'll wear sneakers and casual clothes then.

Justine: And I'll make something a bit fancier than kid food for us for dinner. I'd love to have you stay over. I've discussed with Avery and she's pretty excited to have you around more. No pressure, but I want to put it out there. You're the only guy I would consider having stay over when the romance is so new, but we've known each other forever, so it just seems right.

Emotion swamped him as the words registered deep within. They meant more to him than she would ever know.

Justine: Okay, you went radio-silent. Did I blow it? Damn, I blew it.

Chuckling, he shook his head.

Gary: You didn't blow it. I'm just trying to wrap my brain around the fact I get to spend the day with you both. And the night with you. It might be my ultimate fantasy.

Justine: Um, we need to get you a life, but I'll say thank you because I'm really excited too.

She shot him a geek face emoji.

Breathing a laugh, he texted her goodbye before the dispatcher chimed in over the radio, effectively pulling him back to work.

On Sunday, Gary dressed in sneakers and casual clothes and packed a small bag with some toiletries to take to Justine's. It was a rather warm October day, and he relished the fresh air as he walked to their house. Once there, he knocked on the door and heard Justine yell, "Come in!"

Stepping inside, he closed the door and locked the bottom lock.

"Gary!" Avery called, bounding toward him with a huge grin on her face. Setting his bag on the front table, he picked her up and situated her on his hip.

"Hey, sweetheart. How are you?"

She bit her finger, her eyes awash with excitement. "Good. Mom says you're going to play on the swing set, and in the tree house, and in the sand box with me. They're in the back yard." She pointed toward the back of the house.

Chuckling, he set her on her feet. "I think I can manage that."

"I said he *might* play with us if we ask nicely," Justine said, padding down the hallway. Stopping a few inches from him, she rose to her toes and pecked him on the lips. "Hey," she said softly, a hint of shyness in her tone.

"Hey, hon. You should keep that bottom lock latched when you all are home."

"Noted, Officer Lincoln," she said with a playful salute.

Avery giggled below them, and Justine shot her a lighthearted glare. "And what are you laughing at, missy?"

"You guys kissed. Ew."

"Eh, it's not so bad, kid," Gary said, grinning at Justine. "I really like kissing your mom. I hope that's okay."

Avery gave an excited nod before grabbing his hand. "Come on. I have the sand ready, and we can make sandcastles."

Justine arched a brow. "It's perfectly fine to tell her 'no' and we can sit and have a beer first. It *is* your day off. You might just want to chill for a sec."

Gary's lips curved into a grin. "I'm actually a champion sandcastle creator," he teased. "Lead the way, Avery."

Her resulting beam was everything as she dragged him down the hallway and to the back yard. She had a nice play area with a tall wooden structure that had a fort at the top, two swings attached, and a blue plastic slide, a small sandbox set to the side filled with bright yellow and green buckets, ready to make castles.

Gary took off his shoes and socks and placed them on the patio before following her to the sand box. She was already barefoot, and she jumped into the sand and sat, gesturing for him to follow behind. Once seated, they both began to load sand into the buckets with the shovel.

"Okay, you can have a beer *and* play in the sand," Justine said above him, handing him a chilled bottle. "I think you deserve it."

Chuckling, he grabbed the beer and took a swig. "Thanks."

He and Avery spent some time building some simple but very sturdy castles as Justine sat on the swing and observed them. Every once in a while, she'd chime in with words of encouragement for Avery, reminding him what a great mom she was. Eventually, Avery's attention span waned, and she knocked over one of the sandcastles before snickering.

"The castle has been breached!" Justine called from the swing. "Guess that means it's time for lunch."

"Are we having mac and cheese?" she asked hopefully.

"Always. It's one of the only things you'll eat, so it's a delicacy around here." Rising, she extended her hand and helped Gary stand. "You're so good with her," she whispered, squeezing his hand. "Thank you."

Gary smiled at the admiration in her eyes. "It's nothing, Jus. She's precious. Although, I'm worried if I hang out with you guys too much, I'll get a mac and cheese belly."

Laughing, she shook her head. "I'm not letting that happen. Your body is too hot, Officer Lincoln." Tugging him from the sand box, she led him inside, where Avery was already sitting at their small circular kitchen table.

Their lunch was comfortable, filled with laughter and a plethora of mac and cheese and chicken nuggets. Afterward, Justine urged Avery to take a nap so she would have energy to play with Gary before dinner. Once she was asleep in her room, Justine trailed down the stairs and sat beside Gary on the couch where he was watching football.

"Bribery," she said, snuggling into him as he draped his arm over her shoulder. "Works every time."

"Happy to be of service," he said, placing a kiss on her forehead. "She seems excited to bring me to the tree house before dinner."

"Yep." Justine rested her head on his arm, her eyes roving over his face.

"What is it, hon?"

"We just haven't seen each other for a few days, and now you're here and I've thrust my child in your face. I hope it's not too much for a single guy with no kids."

"Don't be silly. I love her, Jus. And I'm not single anymore, according to Carrie, who seems to have told the entire town we're on the fast track to ending up in an old-age home together."

Laughter bounded from her throat. "I think we knew that would happen. I'm not mad at her though. I'm glad people know. I don't want to draw this out. We care about each other and want to be together, right? I mean, we're not spring chickens anymore. Why waste time playing games?"

"Okay, grandma," he teased, chucking her nose with his finger. "I think you've got a few good years left."

Nuzzling into him, she nodded. "Maybe a few. How are the Steelers doing?"

"Terrible," he said, taking a swig of his beer. "They're not going to make the playoffs at this rate."

"Tell me more about football," she said, trailing a finger over the skin around his throat. "It's so much hotter coming from you in that deep, sexy voice than from my dad and brother."

Chuckling, he detailed her on the game as it progressed until Avery woke up and they headed back outside to play. Gary was given a full tour of Avery's tree house, which Scott had built for her after Justine's divorce, and the three of them played on the swings as the sun set.

Justine made homemade pizzas and meatballs for dinner, although she cheekily admitted she'd picked up the meatballs at the market and only nuked them in sauce. Still, the dinner was fabulous, and Gary sat back once they were done, patting his belly as he slipped into a relaxed food coma. Justine also opened a nice bottle of red, and it only added to his chill mood. Gary realized he felt so comfortable because he'd already established a foundation of friendship and authenticity with his two girls.

"What are you smiling at?" Justine asked, gently nudging him with her toes under the table.

"I'm just realizing how well we all fit together, I guess."

Reaching over, she laced her fingers with his, giving a supportive squeeze.

"Finished," Avery said, pushing her plate away. "Can I have some ice cream?"

"Sure, baby." Rising, she pulled the tub from the freezer and put two scoops in a bowl. "Want some?"

"No way," he said, rubbing his stomach. "I'm stuffed."

"Will you come trick-or-treating with us, Gary?" Avery asked. "It's next week, and Mom says we're going to go with Sebastian, Charlie, and Emily in their neighborhood."

Gary's gaze flew to Justine. "Um...I...is that okay?"

"Uh, yeah," she said as if he were daft, "but the question is, is it okay with *you*? These kids are monsters on Halloween. I'm not sure you're prepared."

He squinted one eye. "Hmmm...criminals or cute kids in costumes?" He lifted one hand above the other and then switched them as if weighing the options. "I think I'll choose the kids."

"I'm not sure how many criminals Ardor Creek has, but I get your point," she muttered. "It's on Thursday night, as you must know. I figured you'd be working."

"I can switch with Jim or Susan. It's up to you." Grabbing a few of the empty plates, he trailed toward the sink to rinse them and put them in her dishwasher.

"Please come, Gary," Avery pleaded before ingesting a spoonful of ice cream.

"The jury has spoken," Justine said, smoothing Avery's hair. "I hope you're ready."

Gary just smiled at her before loading the dishes, wishing she could understand he was thrilled at every chance he got to spend time with them.

Eventually, the sun set, and Justine took Avery upstairs to perform her nightly bedtime ritual. Gary cleaned the kitchen and was wiping down the table when Justine called his name.

Wringing out the cloth, he laid it over the sink and washed his hands before heading upstairs. "Yes?" he asked, pushing Avery's door open.

"She wants you to read to her...if you don't mind. Suddenly, I'm chopped liver over here."

Flashing a grin, he strode over to the bed and took the book Justine thrust his way. She beamed as he began to read, noting how Avery's eyes drooped a little more as each page flipped. When he finished, they stood, and Justine bent down to kiss her on the forehead. "Night, baby."

"Night, Mom. Night, Gary."

"Goodnight, sweetheart," he said, sliding his arm around Justine's shoulders and pulling her into his side. It was a poignant moment for him, and his throat tightened as Justine reached to turn off the lamp. The glow of the nightlight on the far wall guided them as they walked to the door, and Justine left it cracked before they headed downstairs.

"Well, sir," she said, leading him to the kitchen, "you have certainly earned the right to finish this bottle of wine with me." Picking up the half-drunk bottle, she shook it as she bit her lip. "What do you say?"

"Sure," he said, sliding onto the island stool.

She sat beside him, and they savored the wine almost as much as he savored being in her presence, until it grew late, and he felt the first twinge of fatigue.

"Another one bites the dust," she said, lifting the empty bottle. Rising, she chucked it in the recycling container before sauntering toward him. Easing between his thighs, she slid her arms around his neck and gave him a sultry grin. "Well, Officer, I think it's time to go to bed."

His hands glided over her waist, tugging her closer as he nudged her nose with his. "Can we...uh...do things while she's sleeping in the next room?"

Her eyes lit with desire and a bit of mischief. "Yes, but we have to be quiet. As I told you, I wouldn't dream of having anyone else stay over this soon, but it's you. I trust you, Gary, and this is a much different situation than if I were dating someone I'd just met. I know it's probably weird to you, and I'm sorry for that, but I can't ask my brother and my parents to keep her all the time, and I really want to bang you." Grinning, she shrugged. "So, we're going to have to be quiet if that's okay with you."

Pressing his lips to hers, he murmured, "I can be quiet."

Sighing, she gave him a sweet kiss. "Thank god. Let's go upstairs."

Rising from the stool, he followed her down the hallway, grabbing his toiletry bag on the way, and strode up the stairs.

Chapter 13

J ustine led Gary into the small bathroom attached to her bedroom. "I cleared some counter space for you here," she said, gesturing to the white surface beside the sink.

"Thanks," he said, setting his bag down. "I'm going to shed these clothes and give you some privacy." Stepping from the bathroom, he closed the door behind him.

Justine stared at her reflection while brushing her teeth, reminding herself to be patient even though she wanted nothing more than to jump Gary's bones. The lube was stocked and ready to go, and she couldn't wait to use it on him. She also wanted him to feel comfortable being fully naked in front of her and was determined to show him she didn't give a damn about any scars from his injury.

After brushing her teeth and taking care of business, she headed outside to find him scrolling on his phone as he sat on her bed in his underwear. "All yours," she said.

He padded to the bathroom, and she could hear him brushing his teeth behind the closed door as she changed. She slipped on one of her cute PJ sets consisting of a silky tank top and shorts. When he exited the bathroom, his eyes lit with desire when they raked over her.

"I like your PJs," he said, trailing over and sliding an arm around her waist. "Cute and sexy, both at once."

"Thank you, Officer Lincoln. Now, be a good boy and lie on the bed."

His eyebrows lifted. "Man, you're bossy."

Tossing back her head, she laughed. "You're not kidding." She gestured toward the bed, and he followed her directive, lying down and resting the back of his head on the pillow. Justine walked to her bedside table and pulled out a metal container before unscrewing the top and setting it on the surface.

"What's that?"

"This is the lube I was telling you about," she said, lifting it and waggling her eyebrows. "I want to play with you and use it. Are you down with that?"

He slid his hands beneath his head, seeming to contemplate. "I don't mind, but I'd like to make you feel good first."

"I appreciate the sentiment," she said, sitting on the bed, "but our official orgasm count is very uneven, and I'd like to fix that."

Hesitation flashed in his gaze as his lips pursed. "I don't always achieve orgasm, Jus—"

"I know." Placing her palms on the bed on either side of his shoulders, she leaned over him. "But you can't blame a girl for trying." Leaning down, she brushed a kiss over his lips. "Let me try, Gary. I want to make you feel good too."

Lifting a hand, he cupped her jaw. "Okay. My thigh and groin are pretty torn up, Jus. It's not pretty."

"I don't need pretty," she said, straightening and tugging at his underwear. "I just need you to open yourself up to me. We both have to open ourselves if this is going to work."

Expelling a breath, he nodded. Reaching down, he hooked his fingers in the waistband of his boxer briefs and pulled them down before tossing them to the floor. Resting back on the pillow, his eyes assessed her as she gazed at his body.

Justine struggled with the emotion that clogged her throat as she observed his mangled flesh. Red, scarred skin crisscrossed over his thigh and up to his groin area. His shaft lay flat against his upper thigh, and she thanked every god in heaven it hadn't been worse. Lifting her gaze to his, she asked softly, "Can I touch you?"

He nodded.

"Let me ask a better question," she said, scootching to rest on her knees. "Is there anywhere you don't want me to touch you?"

Inhaling deeply, he shook his head. "The surface wounds don't hurt anymore. All my pain is in the muscles underneath. You can touch me anywhere you want."

Her heart railed at the man who'd shot him, and she wished she could go back in time and prevent his pain. "It was a thief at the jewelry store on Main Street, right?"

"Yeah. We shot each other simultaneously, and he died at the scene. I was torn up about it for a while."

"He got what was coming to him," she said, gently placing her palms over his thigh above his knee. "Bastard. If he weren't dead, I'd kill him for doing this to you."

"I appreciate the sentiment, but I don't really want to arrest you for murder again, Jus."

She glowered at him as he teased her. "It would be worth it to save you all the heartache you've gone through from this." Tenderly, she grazed her fingers over the red skin where it met the uninjured smooth skin.

"He was just a kid trying to take care of his family. I don't blame him. We all have our crosses to bear and have to overcome adversity. In the end, I might not be here with you if he hadn't shot me, so I'll take solace in that." Reaching toward her, he smoothed a tuft of hair away from her forehead.

"Man, you are so much more well-adjusted than I am. Teresa would have a field day with you. You could be her poster child for Zen and good karma."

Chuckling, he shrugged. "I've had eight years to deal with my injury. It took a lot of reflection to get here. My fellow officer Chris was shot too, and we did some therapy before returning to the force. He moved to Dallas a few years ago, but we keep in touch. We both tried our best to move on and not let it affect our lives."

Rising on her knees, she placed both hands on his thigh over the scarred skin and began to massage the tender flesh. Gary groaned above her, causing her lips to curve.

"Feel good?"

"Yeah," he rasped, resting his hand behind his head to join the other one. "It throbs a lot, and I try to massage it, but it feels way better when you do it. Especially in that sexy getup."

"Good." Situating herself, she dug into his muscles, hoping it would help ease the pain and also relax him before they crossed over to something sexier. His deep moans urged her on, and she felt a little thrill each time, knowing it felt good.

She eased up his thigh, continuing her ministrations until the back of her hand brushed his shaft. Lifting her eyes to his, she bit her lip. "I'm going to use the lube now. It might get messy."

"Go for it."

Reaching toward the nightstand, she dipped her fingers in the container, gathering the lubricant before sliding her leg over his body and straddling him. Lowering her hands, she placed them on his chest and began to rub small circles over his pecs.

"I didn't realize you were going to start with my chest," he said, grinning as a teasing light glimmered in his eyes.

"I want you to get used to the sensation," she said, smoothing some of the lube over his copper nipples. Gary hissed, sending a shot of arousal to her core. "Oh, yeah, I think you like it."

"Your hands are all over me. What's not to like?"

Eliciting a tiny giggle, she began swirling the lube over his nipples, pleased when they stood to attention under her ministrations.

"It's warm," he murmured.

"Yep. Imagine how it will feel when I go lower."

His resulting growl made her shiver atop his body as he slid his hands from beneath his head and cupped her thighs. His warm palms on her skin drove her wild, and she increased the ministrations on his nipples until he squeezed her legs. "It's working," he said, lifting a brow.

"Oh," she said, understanding dawning as she wriggled atop his thighs. Sure enough, she could feel the slight nudge of his cock as it began to swell beneath her. Drawing her leg back over his body, she balanced on her knees and trailed her hands lower.

After gathering more lubricant from the container, she smoothed it over his scarred thigh and began to massage him again. He groaned, cupping the globe of her ass and squeezing as her fingers inched toward his shaft. Eventually, she reached his semi-hard erection and lifted her gaze to his. Staring deeply into his eyes, she took him in her hand.

Gary sucked in a breath, his hips jutting toward her hand as she gently gripped him. Justine began to jerk him in her hand, sliding her slick palm over his cock. Struggling to catch her breath, she said, "I'm *really* turned on right now."

"Thank god, because I'm drowning in how gorgeous you are, honey."

Overcome with his sweet words, she added her other hand, gripping the base of his shaft as she worked her hand over his rapidly swelling flesh. He jutted into her ministrations, and she licked her lips, dying to take him into her mouth but wondering if it would impede the rhythm she'd established.

"Next time," he said, making the decision for her. "For now, I need you to keep going just like that."

Grinning at how in tune they were, she nodded and continued stroking him, feeling wetness gush between her thighs as his length grew in her grip. His hips undulated, aiding her, and she slid her hand to gently squeeze his balls as her other hand jerked him.

"Oh, god, *yessss*..." he groaned, his head tossing back on the pillow. "I'm going to come soon. Keep doing that."

Unsure which action he was referring to, she continued to gently massage his balls as she stroked his shaft. Moments later, his body tensed, and he moaned her name before his cock began to jerk. Justine watched, mesmerized, as tiny jets of release began to spurt onto his stomach. Slowing the ministrations, she gently tugged his sensitive flesh as he shuddered and trembled beneath her. The muscles of his abdomen quaked as his release spurted to cover them, and he sighed, his head falling limp on the pillow as he squeezed her thigh.

His lips fluttered as he blew out a breath, and she relaxed to sit beside him, gently stroking his uninjured thigh as he recovered. Slowly opening his eyes, he gazed at her, his brown orbs slightly glazed as he traced small circles on her leg.

"That felt good," he murmured.

"I'm glad. It felt good for me too." His features drew together, and she shrugged. "Making you feel good does it for me, Gary. What can I say?"

His lips curved as he ran his palm over her thigh. "It's your turn. Can I use the lube on you too?"

Waggling her brows, she scooted toward the head of the bed and leaned down to rest her lips against his. "I'm counting on it, Officer."

His arms snaked around her, causing her to squeal as he flipped them. Her handsome man straddled her, his flushed body so sexy above hers as he reached toward the nightstand. Pulling some tissues from the box, he wiped the release from his stomach. Setting the tissues on the nightstand, he coated his fingers with lube before settling above her.

"Take off your shirt," he commanded softly.

"Now who's bossy?"

"Justine," he said in a tone both teasing and warning. "Take off your shirt."

Breaking into a grin, she gripped the hem and tugged off the scrap of silk, throwing it to the floor. Gary's eyes brimmed with lust as he touched his slick fingers to the curve of her breast.

"I wonder how the lube will feel against your pretty nipples."

Whimpering, she pushed into his hands. "Don't make me wait to find out."

Her eyes nearly crossed at his sultry smile. Touching his fingers to her nipples, he began to swirl the lube around, causing Justine's body to arch beneath him. After torturing her nipples for what seemed like forever, he commanded her to chuck her skimpy shorts. Once removed, he glided those slick fingers to her core and damn near took her to heaven.

After the marathon round of orgasms, Justine dragged Gary to the shower, where they washed away the evidence of their loving. They scrubbed each other's backs with her pink bath pouf while Gary insisted he would never live it down if the guys at the station knew he'd used the fluffy thing.

Justine rolled her eyes at his teasing, telling him she'd gift wrap a bulk order of fluorescent pink poufs and send them to the station. His reply was a playful swat against her butt, which made her realize she was going to have to threaten him a *lot* more.

They crawled into bed, and she snuggled against his side, already so used to sleeping in the crevices of his body that seemed tailor-made for her. Wriggling against him, she gently rubbed his chest, loving the feel of the scratchy hairs against her fingertips.

"That was fun," she said before yawning.

"So fun. And very sexy."

"Mm-hmm," was her soft reply as her eyes drooped. "Thank you for today. Avery loves you so much."

"She's adorable like her mama," he said, stroking her hair. "And no 'thank yous,' remember? Neither of us need those, Jus. Not anymore."

Tears stung her eyes as she realized—for perhaps the first moment in her life—what it truly meant to be cared for by a man. She'd never experienced one ounce of the admiration and respect from Dean that Gary gave her in spades. Grateful for him and their close bond, she held him tight, pretty sure she was already halfway in love with him. *True* love, the likes of which she thought she had with Dean but had never really achieved.

Overcome with joy, she reveled in the feeling as she held her man close in the dark.

Chapter 14

Gary switched shifts with Jim on Thursday so he could go trick-or-treating with his girls. They loaded into Justine's car and drove to Peter and Carrie's house, where she was taking pictures of Sebastian, Charlie, and Emily in their costumes on the front lawn.

"Oh, good, you're here," Carrie said, waving them over. "Let's get some pictures of Avery in her costume and with the kids."

Avery bounded over, and Carrie snapped away on her phone as she and Justine oohed and aahed at how cute the kids were. Sebastian was an astronaut, Charlie was a cowboy, Emily was a fairy, and Avery was a princess—which Justine informed him she was every year, and she'd given up on suggesting other options.

"Hey, man," Peter said, trailing toward him and handing him a beer. "You're going to need this."

Gary smiled and took the bottle, clinking it with Peter's iced tea before they drank.

Giving him a droll look, Peter murmured, "You must really want to get into Justine's pants to sign up for Halloween."

Chuckling at his lifelong friend, Gary patted him on the back. "You're not fooling anyone, Peter. Carrie's got you whipped, and you love spending time with the kids. Just admit it."

Narrowing his eyes, he contemplated. "Maybe. I do like it when Carrie plays dress-up, if you know what I mean. She bought this sexy witch outfit the other day—"

"TMI, buddy," Gary said, holding up his hand. "But I'm glad you all are keeping it spicy or whatever."

"Wait 'til you're married again. I know you, Gary. You'll have a ring on her finger by Christmas," he said, gesturing to Justine. "You and Nicole were inseparable from the day you met."

"I'm not sure that's the best example," Gary muttered, taking a sip of beer. "But I am kind of crazy about Jus. I have been for a while."

His friend's blue eyes assessed him. "Why did you hold back? She's been single for a while."

Sighing, he rubbed the back of his neck. "Long story. I had some...reservations that I wouldn't...I don't know...make her happy or whatever."

"That's ridiculous, man. If Carrie can forgive me for all the shit I put her through, you're probably a candidate for man of the year."

"I'm happy you guys figured it out," Gary said, lifting his beer in a salute. "You two were always meant to be together. And as far as me and Jus...well, I was probably scared for nothing. She's so damn accepting. It's one of the things I love most about her."

"Well, hot damn," Peter said, raising an eyebrow, "we're already at the 'love' stage." He made quotation marks with his fingers. "You move fast, bro."

"Sorry I said anything," Gary said, scowling. "Don't blow up my spot, okay? I don't want to scare her away."

"Your secret is safe with me. Don't tell my wife though. She'll announce it from Abby's mayoral pulpit if she finds out you're in *loooooove.*"

Carrie finished taking the pictures and strode over to them, handing Peter the phone. "Can you look over the pictures and pick out the best ones? I told Ashlyn, Teresa, and Abby I'd send them over."

"I don't really have an eye for that stuff, honey—"

"Where did I put that costume I ordered online?" she interrupted, rubbing her chin as she squinted at the sky. "The special one for when we get home tonight? Guess I won't be able to look for it since I'll have to be looking through pictures—"

"Fine, woman," Peter said, shooting her a glare. "I'll look through the pictures. You drive a hard bargain."

"Thank you." Lifting to her toes, she kissed his cheek.

Peter snaked his arm around her waist and placed a long, lingering kiss on her lips.

Drawing back, she sighed. "As much as I want to make out with you, we have to get this show on the road. And it would probably gross out Gary." She flashed him a grin. "Let's roll out in five minutes."

The men nodded in acknowledgment, and Gary helped Peter filter through the pictures to find the best ones. Eventually, they began their journey around the neighborhood, the kids with their bright orange pumpkin baskets in hand. Carrie and Justine held their daughters' hands until Avery tugged hers away and stated she was big enough to join the boys, who didn't need as much supervision.

Justine fell into step beside Gary and slid an arm around his waist. "Well?" she asked, lifting her brows. "Is it torture?"

"I'm having fun," he said, encircling her waist and pulling her close. "Thanks for including me."

"Wait until they're hopped up on a thousand candy bars. I'm already dreading bedtime tonight."

"If you need me to help with any sort of bribery, I'm in."

Her eyes lit with mischief. "Oh, that's awesome. I can work with that." They walked a few steps before she sighed as she gazed at the kids in the distance approaching their next house.

"What's wrong?"

"My baby isn't a baby anymore, and I'm so sad about it." She tilted her head to gaze into his eyes. "I think I want another baby, Gary. Shit. I just said it out loud. If you want to freak, that's perfectly acceptable."

Gary's heart thrummed as he digested her statement. Anxiety he couldn't give her what she craved gnawed at him, and he figured it was best to be honest. "I'm not sure this is the best time to discuss this—"

"I know," she said, waving a hand. "Still so new. I shouldn't have said anything."

"I don't mind, Jus," he said, shaking his head. "It's just that...well, I'm not sure I can have kids...with the injury and all."

"Ohh," she said, awareness crossing her features. "Did it hinder your ability to have kids?"

"Definitely in some capacity. The thing is, it's not really something the doctors could quantify unless I tried, and Nicole and I never tried."

White teeth toyed with her lip as she pondered. "I see."

"I'm sorry if this is too much. I just want to be honest with you."

"I'm the one who brought it up," she said, giving him a reassuring grin. "Let's table it for now and revisit it in the future. We can always discuss it down the road, right?"

"Right."

"Good. In the meantime, let's enjoy tonight. How cute are the kids in their costumes?"

"They're adorable."

Lowering her hand, she slid her palm over his and laced their fingers. "Thank you for coming."

Leaning down, he placed a reverent kiss on her lips. "Thank you for inviting me. I like being included in your activities with Avery. I know it's not easy to bring someone else in."

"It wasn't until you."

Taken by her words, he squeezed her hand as they continued to the next house, realizing he hadn't known how much he wanted a family until his girls had allowed him into theirs.

Chapter 15

J ustine fell into a smooth pattern with Gary, overcome with how easy it was to just *be* with him. It probably shouldn't have been a surprise since they'd been friends for years, but her former relationship hadn't given her the warm and fuzzies about love. Still, she opened her heart to her new lover and was rewarded each time he gave her that sexy smile or held her in his strong arms.

He began to stay over a few nights a week as they eased Avery into the new situation. She took to it like a fish to water since she'd already adored Gary before their relationship turned romantic. The crisp fall days turned to chilly, shorter ones, and before Justine knew it, the holidays were around the corner.

Two weeks before Thanksgiving, Justine received a call from Teresa.

"Hey, Teresa, what's up?" she chimed, tapping the speaker button so she could continue to paint the canvas in her shed.

"Hey. You sound busy. Want me to call you back?"

"No, it's fine," she said, stroking the brush over the right side of the painting. "One of Kristoff's rich friends in the city commissioned an abstract painting from me, and I want to get it done this week. He liked one of my other paintings in the New York gallery but wanted one tailor-made for him. Must be nice to be so rich you can snap your fingers and get a custom painting, huh?"

Her chuckle wafted over the phone. "Seriously. That says a lot about your talent though. Nice job."

"Thanks. Anyway, I can paint and chat at the same time."

"As you know, the group always gets together each Thanksgiving at Scott and Ashlyn's house, and we loved having you and Avery last year. This year, they're going to invite Gary too, and we figured you'd all come together."

Elation swam through her veins at the notion she had been accepted into their tight friend group after her divorce. "That's awesome. I'd love to. Is Mark mad I stole all his friends?" she asked, snickering.

"I'm not sure *stole* is the right word, but he loves you, Justine, and is happy you're forging ahead in this new life you're fashioning. Ashlyn was going to call you and ask you all to come, but it gave me an opportunity to check in and see how things are going with Gary."

"Sneaky," Justine said, feeling her lips curve. "It's going very well, thank you very much."

"I'm so glad. It's really beautiful to see you both opening up to each other considering your histories and his injury."

"I think he's the one, Teresa. The *real* one this time. You know I like to plow full steam ahead, so I'm trying not to do something stupid like blurt out how obsessed I am with him and ask him to move in with me. He says he wants to buy a house, so it's a discussion we'll have to have soon." Silence crackled over the phone before Justine sighed. "Okay, give it to me. I'm sensing you have something you want to say."

"I do, but I don't want to overstep."

"Overstep away. I can handle it."

After a pause, she said, "I think moving in together is the next step, and I'm on board with that. But I think you should contemplate selling your house and looking for a house you and Gary could buy together."

Justine mulled as the idea took hold in her brain. "Because of Dean?"

"Yes. Your current house holds a lot of past trauma and bad memories. I understand why you stayed in the house after the divorce. It belonged to you after the settlement, and you were just starting your business. But now you're making more, and combined with Gary's income, you both could find a house where you could start fresh. I know it's still early, but it never hurts to float the idea. Buying a house takes months and even years sometimes, so I don't think it's too shocking to discuss with him."

Chewing her lip, Justine contemplated. "It's not the worst idea. I do hate the energy of this house, but your reasons are spot-on as to why I stayed."

"It makes perfect sense, but there's power in moving on to something new and better."

Grinning, she fisted her hand on her hip. "Are you charging by the hour for this? It's good stuff."

Laughter bounded over the phone. "Never."

"By the way, Gary is so damn Zen or whatever. I can't wait for you to spend more time with him. He's got this calm, centered view of his injury and doesn't hold any anger or resentment. I'd probably rail at the world."

"He likely received some therapy after his injury as a require-ment to return to work, but some people are just resilient by nature. I'd love to hear more about it, but I don't want to make him uncomfortable."

"He did mention the station set him up with therapy before going back in the field. He's always been a bit shy, but if you bring it up to him when you two are alone, he might chat about it with you. Anyway, it's just something I find really cool about him."

"That's wonderful, Justine. I think you two are perfect for each other."

Justine resisted the urge to squeal like a teenager with a crush. "Me too."

"Anyway, I don't want to interrupt your work, so I'll inform you that Scott and Ashlyn are asking everyone to arrive around two o'clock on Thanksgiving. That will give the kids some time to play in the back yard before we eat—and time for us to drink some pre-dinner wine too." She breathed a laugh. "Scott will call Gary to ask him directly. Hope you're ready for your first holiday meal with the gang as an official couple."

"Bring it on," she said, chucking her eyebrows. "Thanks so much, Teresa. Can't wait."

Justine tapped the phone and ended the call. A few minutes later, it rang again, and she swiped her finger across the screen and tapped the speaker icon.

"Hey, Ashlyn."

"Hey, you. So, I know Teresa called you, but I still wanted to formally invite you, so consider this your official invitation to Thanksgiving."

Smiling, Justine nodded. "She did, and thank you. I know I came last year with Avery, but this will be different since I'm technically coupled-up, I guess."

"Will it ever. I've already made Scott promise he and the guys will play soccer with the kids so we can grill you."

"Great," Justine muttered. "At least there will be booze."

Ashlyn's melodious laugh drifted over the phone. "That there will. Just bring some wine or champagne and that's enough of a contribution. I'll obviously cook, but we'll have most of the food prepped by the time everyone arrives so I can join the inquisition."

"Yikes," Justine said, grinning. "I'll bring lots of wine. Excited to see you, Ashlyn."

"Me too, sweetie. Take care."

Justine worked on the painting for a few more hours until it was time to pick up Avery from school. On the way to the car, she noticed Jeremy strolling down his driveway.

"Hey, neighbor," she called, waving.

"Hey there. You heading out?"

"Yep. Picking up Avery from school. You?"

"I'm doing the same for the girls."

Nearing her car, she halted and tilted her head. "You know, we should probably combine our efforts since we live next door to each other. We could do our small part to save the planet and carpool with the kids."

His eyebrows lifted as he pondered. "I'd be happy to. Jenny and I debated having them take the bus, but we both work from home and enjoy driving them. I wouldn't mind having an afternoon off here or there though. She and I alternate custody every week now that we're all in the same area."

"Let's put together a plan then," she said, opening her door and leaning on it with her arm. "I'm happy to meet Jenny and show her I'm not a serial killer. I did get arrested for attempted murder but was exonerated, and I assure you, I am a model citizen."

Rubbing his chin, he squinted at the sky. "I think you just gave me my idea for my next thriller. Small-town mom terrorizes town before they forgive her and she becomes the carpool organizer."

Tossing back her head, Justine roared with laughter. "I'd read that as soon as it was released. I want a cut though." She lifted her finger.

"Done. I'll talk to Jenny and set up a time for you to meet her. In the meantime, don't tailgate me."

Sliding into the car, she called, "I've got a head start, so I think *you'll* have to worry about tailgating me. Bye!" Giving a wave, she closed the door and headed to pick up Avery.

Once home, Justine cooked spaghetti for dinner as she waited for Gary to arrive. Little butterflies of anticipation flitted in her stomach, and she grinned at what a romantic dope she was.

Avery was in her room playing on her tablet when Justine heard the front door open and close. Footsteps padded down the hall-way, and she grinned as she stirred the sauce in the large pot over the stove.

"Well, Officer Lincoln, you're here earlier than I thought—"

Breath rushed from her lungs as an arm encircled her neck, cutting off her air supply as she struggled to breathe. Dropping the wooden spoon, she clawed the arm as terror ripped through her veins.

"You fucking *whore*," Dean breathed in her ear, tugging her against his body as the smell of alcohol pervaded her nostrils. "I know you've been fucking that asshole cop who helped you get the restraining order against me. I'm not scared of him, Justine."

Struggling with all her might, she kicked his shin with her heel, wishing she was still wearing her sneakers to increase the strength of the blow. He grimaced but held tight, and a wave of nausea overtook her due to his stale, vodka-ridden breath.

"I want to see Avery. Where is she?"

"You'll never see her again," she gritted, gripping his arm with both hands and digging her nails into his skin. "You gave up that right!"

"She's my daughter!" he yelled, his words slurred and angry. "Frannie wants to meet her, and you won't keep her from me any longer."

Reaching for the knife block, Justine strained to grab one of the knives to use as a weapon. Dean's sinister chuckle sounded in her ear as she whimpered.

"Not this time, Jus. I learned my lesson last time you tried to stab me, you vicious bitch!"

Justine closed her eyes, deciding to muster all her strength and jab her elbow into his side. If she did it hard enough, perhaps he would lose his grip and she could free herself. Steeling herself, she gritted her teeth and prepared to let loose.

Suddenly, Dean grunted and flew away from her body as if he were being dragged into a tornado. Whirling around, Justine held her hands to her burning throat and observed Gary, his hands clenched around the fabric of Dean's shirt as he hauled him toward her back door. Dean threw a wild punch, which Gary caught in his fist, twisting Dean's arm before landing a striking jab in his abdomen. Dean doubled over, coughing and sputtering before Gary grabbed him and tugged him through the back door.

Once outside, he heaved Dean toward the grass. Her ex-husband spun around and charged, but he was no match for Gary's training and skill. He caught him by the shoulders and surged his knee into Dean's nose. Dean's head snapped back before he rested it in his hands and screamed. Stepping forward, Gary grabbed him by his thick hair and landed a solid blow to the man's jaw. He collapsed on the grass and curled into a ball as his nose bled.

"Are you okay?" Justine rasped, jogging toward them and clutching Gary's shoulder.

"Yeah," he said, wiping his arm over his lips. Something primal welled in Justine's solar plexus, and she realized it was some sort of base response at Gary's protection. She would have time later to digest why she was so turned on by him beating the shit out of her ex-husband, but holy hell, it was hot. Swallowing thickly, she watched him pull his phone from his pocket and dial 911 before lifting it to his ear.

"Avery's upstairs?" he asked, his eyes glazed with anger as Dean sputtered on the ground.

"Yes," she said, glancing toward her bedroom window. "I should go check on her."

"Go," he said with a nod before speaking into the phone. "Hey, Gail, I've got a restraining order violation in action. Send backup to 268 Maple Street, stat."

Justine grasped his hand and squeezed. "Thank you," she whispered.

"I've wanted to do that for a long time," he said, glowering at Dean. "I'm just sorry I wasn't here sooner."

"You were perfect." Lifting to her toes, she kissed his cheek. "Be back in a sec."

Rushing inside, she trailed down the hallway and up the stairs to find Avery sitting on her bed with her pink tablet, headphones over her ears as she watched a cartoon. Thanking every god in heaven she hadn't heard the altercation, Justine sat on the bed.

"Hey, Mom," she said, pausing the cartoon and taking off her earphones. "Is dinner ready?"

"It will be soon, baby," she said, scootching closer and drawing her into a tight hug. "I just needed to hug you really hard. Hope that's okay."

Avery's tiny arms squeezed her, and she fought back tears. Kissing her blond hair, she asked, "Your dad hasn't ever tried to see you at school, right?"

Avery shook her head before drawing back. "You said he wasn't going to see me anymore."

"He's not." She smoothed her hand over the golden tresses. "I'm just making sure. If he tries to see you, or if you see him, I want you to tell me, okay?"

Worry entered her blue eyes. "Okay."

"I don't mean to scare you," she said, trying to sound cheerful. "There's nothing to worry about. Remember what I said once Dad and I got divorced?"

"You'll do the worrying, and I'll do the kid stuff."

"That's right. Worrying is for adults, and it's not fun. I need you to be a kid and remind me to have fun. We've both got very important jobs to do."

Beaming, she said, "I like to have fun."

"Me too. Spaghetti will be ready in thirty minutes. In the meantime, I want you to stay upstairs. Some of Gary's police friends are stopping by, and that will be boring, so I'll let you have some extra time on the tablet."

"Yay!" she cheered, eyes lighting with excitement.

"For tonight only, young lady." Standing, she kissed her forehead. "I'll come get you once it's time to come downstairs. Enjoy your cartoon."

"Thanks, Mom." Settling back against the pillows, she put back on her headset, and Justine drew a deep, calming breath. Trailing back downstairs, she glanced through the window and noticed the police cruiser parked in front of her house. Heading to the back yard, she stepped outside to find a bloody-nosed Dean in handcuffs as Gary's fellow patrol officer Susan Ludwig took notes.

"And he was assaulting her when you arrived?" Susan asked, her face impassive as she scribbled on the paper.

"Yep. Had her in a choke hold. Probably would've strangled her if I hadn't shown up."

Nodding, Susan glanced Justine's way and gave a brief smile. She was a stoic woman, and Justine remembered she'd graduated a few years before Mark. She was an Ardor Creek lifer and a staple on the police force. Susan had also been one of the officers on the scene the night Justine was arrested for attempted murder.

"Hey, Susan," Justine said, walking to stand beside Gary and rubbing her arms. "I guess you need a statement."

"She invited me over!" Dean yelled, struggling to yank his arms out of the handcuffs. "She's a lying bitch."

"Mr. Rodgers, I'd shut up if I were you," Susan said, holding up a hand. "You are in direct violation of a restraining order."

"Fuck you," Dean muttered.

Susan strode over and encircled his arm before dragging him across the lawn. "I can help you, Susan," Gary said.

"Nope," she said, shaking her head. "You're not on duty, and I don't want to violate protocol. Let me shove this jerk in the car and I'll come back and take your statement, Justine."

Gary nodded as Justine approached him. Gliding her arms around his waist, she buried her face in his chest and squeezed so tight she probably mashed his organs together.

"You're okay, hon," he said, smoothing his hand over her hair. "I'm here."

"Avery didn't see or hear anything, thank god."

"That's good." He paused for a moment. "Is it too soon for me to scold you for not having the door locked?"

Lifting her head, she stared into his eyes. "How do you know I didn't have the door locked?" His brows lifted, and she breathed a laugh. "Busted. You'd think I'd learn my fucking lesson. I've always felt so safe in Ardor Creek, and I just never made it a habit to lock the door when I'm home. Do I get an award for biggest idiot in town?"

Chuckling, he swiped the hair off her forehead. "We just need to make it a habit. That's all, Jus."

Her eyes darted over his face as she pondered. "Teresa says I should move out of this house. That it has bad energy."

His expression turned contemplative. "It's not the worst idea."

Justine bit her lip. "In the tradition of continuing our 'way too soon' conversations, she also suggested we should look for a house together. I mean, if you want to buy one and I want to sell this one, we could pool our resources and find one together that my shithead ex-husband hasn't lived in."

Gary's full lips formed a slow, sexy smile. "Are you asking me to buy a house with you, Jus?"

"Noooo," she said, although her tone was teasing. "I'd never dream of it this soon. But if you sent me some listings and I sent you some, we could just get an idea of what we like. It doesn't hurt to send each other listings, right?"

He huffed a laugh and shook his head. "I guess not."

"Then it's settled. We'll ping each other with listings we like. Don't make it weird, okay? Just two normal people who aren't discussing buying a house after dating a few weeks."

"But being friends for years," he said, gently running the backs of his fingers over her jaw.

"Really good friends," she confirmed, rising to her toes and pecking his lips. "In fact, I'd like to show you how friendly I can be later, after all this crap dies down. You beating the shit out of my ex-husband *really* turned me on, Officer."

"That's probably all sorts of wrong, but I just don't give a damn," he said, chuckling.

Susan returned to take Justine's statement before assuring her Dean would spend the night in jail. Gary and Justine thanked her before she drove away with Dean in the back seat.

Justine warmed up the spaghetti sauce again and threw in the noodles. They had dinner around the small table as Justine assessed her mood. She wasn't as shaky as she'd been when Dean attacked her in the past, and she attributed that to two things. One, she was a hell of a lot fiercer now and had really grown into her strength and mental fortitude. Second, she had Gary by her side, and he was such a steady, calming presence in her life. Focusing back on her dinner companions, she couldn't contain her grin as she watched Gary question Avery about her day at school.

"So, that's it, really," Avery said, shrugging. "Mrs. Valentino says I'm really good at three-digit addition and subtraction. We're going to start learning multiplication soon, and she thinks I'm going to rock it."

"Mrs. Valentino is very supportive," Justine said, resting her chin on her fist as her elbow sat atop the table. "Avery is flourishing in her class. I'm so glad she's her teacher."

"Me too," Avery said, beaming from spaghetti-stained lips.

"Please use your napkin," Justine said, handing it to her.

Her daughter scowled before wiping off the sauce.

Gary took the moment to lift a forkful of spaghetti to his lips and spread the sauce around. Avery snickered before Justine thrust a napkin in his face.

"You too, young man."

Gary winked before taking the napkin and wiping away the sauce. Once dinner was finished and the kitchen was clean, they read to Avery before she fell asleep. When they finally entered

Justine's bedroom, she was exhausted. Gary approached her, concern in his deep brown eyes as his gaze darted over her throat.

"You're bruised here," he said softly, running his fingers over her neck. "Fuck, I should've killed him."

"It's over," she said, sliding her arms around his neck. "I don't want to talk about him ever again. Hopefully, they'll lock him up for a while for violating the restraining order. It's also clearly stated in our divorce settlement that he has no visitation rights with Avery. He said his new flame wants to meet her. That's why he showed up tonight."

"Over my dead body. I'll make sure he gets everything in the book thrown at him. It will be my first priority when I get to work tomorrow."

"Thank you," she said, kissing him before releasing his neck to change into a comfy tank top. "I hope this isn't a letdown, because I was ready to jump your bones two hours ago, but now the adrenaline has worn off, I kind of just want to lie down and have you hold me. Is that lame?"

"Not at all. I'm beat too, hon."

Once they'd prepped for bed, they slid between the sheets, and Gary pulled her close. He stroked her hair as she caressed the spiky hairs on his chest, and she brought up the impending holiday.

"Scott called you about Thanksgiving, right?"

"Yep. I'm down. We can drive together if that works."

"Works for me."

"I told my parents I'd do Thanksgiving here and fly down to see them for Christmas."

Her lips formed a pout at the thought of not spending Christmas with him. "Do they ever come back here to visit you?"

"Not really. They don't like the cold weather, and it's easier for me to travel to them."

"Bummer. I really wanted to spend Christmas with you. Just add it to the 'moving too fast/freak-out' list of things I'm throwing your way."

Laughter rumbled in his chest. "I want to spend it with you too, hon. Maybe next year, if we're still going strong, we could fly to Florida to see them. We could take Avery to Disney World."

Lifting her head, she couldn't stop her lips from forming a huge grin. "You know that offering to take a woman's kid to Disney World is, like, the sexiest thing on the planet to a mom, right?"

Amusement crossed his expression. "I thought you all were more into Henry Cavill and the hot guys who make up *The Avengers*."

She gave a "*pfft*" and waved her hand. "Avengers, shma-vengers. Help me navigate Disney World with my spawn and you've cemented your place between my legs for eternity."

Tossing back his head on the pillow, he broke into joyful laughter. "Who knew that's all it took? I have some single buddies I need to share this info with."

"Share away," she said, snuggling back into his chest. "It's good stuff."

Their bodies relaxed as their breathing grew heavy, and Justine grinned when he slid his hand down her back and cupped her butt. There was something possessive in the gesture as he clutched her to his body. Lulled by his strong, steady heartbeat, she allowed sleep to claim her as she let go of the events of the day.

<h1 style="text-align:center">Chapter 16</h1>

J ustine, Gary, and Avery drove together to Scott and Ashlyn's house on Thanksgiving. Once there, Justine thrust a bag filled with wine and prosecco at Ashlyn.

"Wow," Ashlyn said, taking it and lifting it to test its weight. "When I said bring wine, I meant a bottle or two."

"Well, you said you were going to grill me, so I wanted to be prepared," Justine said, giving a cheeky grin before hugging her.

"Love it. Let me open a bottle and we can go out back. Carrie's crew is already here, and Peter and Scott are playing soccer with them. You can join them if you want, guys," she said to Avery and Gary.

Gary's eyes narrowed. "Should I be worried about this questioning thing?" he asked, rubbing the back of his neck.

"Not in the least," Ashlyn said, trailing toward the fridge and pulling out a juice box and a can of beer. After popping the beer, she handed it to Gary and put the straw in the juice box before handing it to Avery. "Go forth and kick many goals. Have fun!"

"Thank you, Ashlyn," Avery said.

"You're welcome, sweetheart."

Avery bounded out the back door, and Gary leaned down to kiss Justine. "Don't share all my secrets."

"Wouldn't dream of it," she said, mimicking zipping her lips shut.

He followed Avery out the door, and Justine chatted with Ashlyn as she opened the prosecco. Once they had full glasses, they headed outside to join Carrie on the back porch.

"Hey, Justine," Carrie said, rising to hug her before they lowered into the chairs that circled the stone patio. "First, a toast to yet another Thanksgiving together. I love our friend family so much."

They clinked their glasses and took a sip before Carrie continued.

"So, I don't want to pry—"

"That's a first," Ashlyn murmured.

Carrie shot her a glare. "I heard about Dean breaking into your home, Jus. My god, you must have been terrified. I'm so glad you're okay."

"It was surreal," Justine said, shaking her head. "I think I'd begun to feel safe because I hadn't seen him in so long. And then, he was strangling me, and all the old memories and fear flooded back."

"I'm so sorry, Justine," Ashlyn said, gripping her hand and giving a supportive squeeze. "From what I hear from our resident gossip,"—her eyes playfully skated to Carrie—"Gary swooped in and saved the day."

"Oh my god, guys," Justine said wistfully, leaning back in her chair. "He beat the ever-loving shit out of him. It wasn't even a contest. I'm not gonna lie about the fact it set my lady parts on fire."

Carrie snickered against the back of her hand. "It sounds hot."

"So hot." Taking a deep breath, she continued. "Honestly, I guess I'd become complacent, thinking my issues with Dean were over. I just need to be more careful in the future."

"Sometimes, the universe gives us a reminder to watch out for ourselves," Ashlyn said. "I'm just so glad he didn't hurt you or Avery."

"Me too. She has no idea he was even there. We were really lucky."

"Sooooo, it might be a good idea to have Gary around all the time, right?" Carrie asked, biting her lip. "Like maybe making it more permanent and moving in? I mean, the man did voluntarily sign up for trick-or-treating. He might be a saint."

Chuckling, Justine nodded. "Truth. He and I have started talking about looking for a house together since he wants to buy one and I want to sell the one I'm in. I'm just worried to move too fast.

What if he wakes up one day and regrets the fact he's saddled with a partner and kid? I don't want to freak him out."

"Uh, I think that's what he signed up for with you," Carrie said with a teasing eye roll. "It's different when you've known someone for years before dating. I think you can move a *bit* faster, right?"

"Don't ask me," Justine said, waving her hand. "I am the last person anyone should ask about relationships."

Ashlyn cleared her throat before asking softly, "Do you love him, Justine?"

Sighing, Justine felt her lips curve. "I'm pretty sure I do. How crazy is that? My brother's friend who I've known forever. But we were both married to someone else, so I never thought of him that way...until I did."

"So romantic," Carrie breathed.

"But I'm intent on doing things right this time. I can't afford to make mistakes. I fucked up so many things in my marriage, and I won't do that again."

Ashlyn's lips pursed. "I think you're going to make mistakes even if you try not to. That's part of being human."

"Maybe," she said, shrugging. "But I'm going to do my best to limit them. Avery deserves that. Hell, I deserve that. And Gary deserves to be with someone who has her shit together. If we do take this all the way, it's the last time. I don't want another divorce for either of us. I want us to be sure."

"That's fair," Carrie said, wrinkling her nose. "But don't hold back just because you're intent on doing things perfectly. Take it from me," she said, gazing across the yard to where Peter and the kids were playing soccer, "it rarely works. I was so adamant I wouldn't let Peter hurt me again that I kept Sebastian from him for ten years." Lowering her gaze, she shook her head. "It was a terrible mistake, and I can't make up lost time. Learn from my fuck ups, Justine."

"Uh, I think we all have enough fuck ups here to last a lifetime," Ashlyn said, lifting her glass. "So, let's just do the best we can with what we've got." Leaning forward, they clinked their glasses as Mark and Teresa appeared.

"Did I hear something about fucking up?" Mark asked, grinning as he held Rose in the carrier. "I'm the poster child for that, right, hon?" He grinned at Teresa.

"Never," she said, rising to her toes to peck him on the cheek. "Did I miss the wine portion of the day?"

"Oh, honey, we're just getting started," Ashlyn said, rising. "Grant is happily playing soccer with the crew, and Carly is sleeping," she said, referencing her almost one-year-old daughter. "Mommy did the cooking, and Dad is on child duty." She pointed to Scott as he kicked the ball to Avery. "Who needs another round?"

"Me!" the ladies all said in unison, lifting their hands.

Sliding her arm around Teresa's shoulders, Ashlyn led her inside to grab a glass of wine as Justine smiled at her brother. "Leave Rosie here, and you can go play with the kids."

Scowling, Mark set the carrier on the patio. "I'd berate you for calling her that, but I'm thankful for the free babysitting." Kissing her on the forehead, he jogged off to join the revelry.

"He hates it when I call her that," Justine said, leaning down to brush a finger over Rose's soft cheek as she slept. "Man, she's so freaking cute."

"Peter is on Emily duty," Carrie said, gazing off in the distance as Peter chased their two-year-old daughter around the yard. "I'm not going to deny it's sexy as hell."

"When did we become domesticated saps?" Justine asked, snickering.

"No idea. Let's get tipsy and talk about how cute our men are. But we can't ever tell them. It will ruin our stern mommy reputations." She made an "X" over her heart.

Grinning, Justine nodded and downed the rest of her prosecco, figuring she could talk about how sweet and sexy Gary was all day long.

Thanksgiving dinner was lovely, filled with lots of laughter, food, and wine, and by the time things wound down, Gary was ready to head home with his girls and relax before his early shift in the morning. While the ladies were cleaning the kitchen—which was code for drinking the last of the wine—the guys sat in the living room watching football. Avery strode into the room, glancing at Mark, who held a sleeping Rose in his arms, before approaching Gary. Opening his arms, Gary let her crawl into his lap, holding her as she rested her head on his shoulder.

"You tired, sweetheart?" he asked, stroking her soft hair.

She nodded against his shirt.

Mark cleared his throat before breaking into a huge grin. "I think she likes you better than me. Man, I'm jealous."

"I love you, Uncle Mark," she mumbled sleepily, "and I love Gary too."

Gary's heart swelled to the size of a damn ocean as he held her tight. "I love you too," he said, placing a kiss on her head.

He and Mark chatted throughout the game before Justine rolled in, flashing a grin as she observed her sleeping daughter. "I'm ready to go when you are."

Nodding, Gary stood, holding Avery tight as he said goodbye to his buddies. Ashlyn appeared, hugging him before he and Justine slipped out the door. Carefully, he placed Avery in the backseat before offering to drive. Justine handed him the keys and slipped into the passenger seat.

"Well, we survived our first holiday together," she said softly. "It was a really nice day. And if this one keeps sleeping, we can have a *really* nice evening." She waggled her eyebrows. "And I also have something awesome to tell you."

"What's that?"

"Carrie agreed to watch Avery next Saturday so we can have an adult night together."

"Is that so?" he asked, reaching over to thread his fingers with hers. "Because I'd really like to take you on a date, Justine."

"Aw, that's so sweet. I was thinking more along the lines of you finally using those handcuffs on me for sexy times, but you can take me on a date first, I guess."

Chuckling, Gary nodded. "Okay, I'll pick a place. Anything you don't like?"

"If it has food and alcohol, I'm in. Just nowhere with kids meals."

Breathing a laugh, he squeezed her hand. "You got it."

"And you'll bring the handcuffs?"

Gary smiled as he contemplated her request. They had been trying several things in the bedroom and working up to the eventual moment he would hopefully be able to seal the deal. The various methods they'd tried so far, including the lubrication, oral stimulation, and massages, had been fantastic, but he hadn't been able to reach orgasm while making love. Justine was extremely patient and always assured him she enjoyed everything they tried together, but he was dying to reach the next level.

Thankfully, he now felt comfortable with her, and he'd always been into a little light bondage, so maybe employing the handcuffs was a good idea. Perhaps it would give him that extra stimulation he needed to reach the peak with her.

"I'll bring the handcuffs," he said in a low tone.

Justine visibly shivered as desire flashed in her eyes. "And that deep sexy voice. Bring the handcuffs and that voice, and we're going to set the damn bed on fire."

He shot her a playful glance. "I like your enthusiasm. I hope I can live up to it."

"Every time you touch me, it feels amazing. You have to know that by now."

Lifting her hand, he kissed it as he turned into her driveway. "I hope so, hon. I love making you feel good."

After parking the car, he lifted Avery in his arms and carried her up the stairs, realizing he was actually anticipating next week's sexy shenanigans after their date. Gary hadn't positively anticipated sex in so long, and he attributed it all to his patient, thoughtful partner. Nicole had assured him there would be someone out there who would accept him exactly as he was. Never in a million years had Gary allowed himself to dream it would be Justine.

As he put Avery to bed, he thanked his lucky stars, realizing the universe might have realized it owed him some good karma after the past few years. If so, he was extremely thankful.

Justine leaned over and tucked Avery in before straightening and extending her hand. Sliding his palm over hers, he rose and

stared into her limitless eyes as she grinned up at him. *I love you.*
The words rested on the tip of his tongue, dying to spring free, but
he knew it was too soon. So, he kissed her forehead, reveling in
her gorgeous smile before following her to bed.

Chapter 17

Gary made reservations at the fancy new Mediterranean restaurant that had recently opened in Battle Falls for their date. As much as he loved Ardor Creek, he figured a change of scenery would be nice, and it would prevent people from stopping by their table to chat. Such was the way in small towns, and he selfishly wanted to Justine all to himself.

When he arrived to pick her up, dressed in his crisp collared shirt, black slacks, and dress shoes, he knocked on her door, completely unprepared for the sight that awaited him. Drawing open the door, she stepped outside in a deep blue dress that fell to her knees above blue high heels. Her hair was also dyed a light shade of blue, and she looked like a sexy fairy he wanted to whisk away and ravish. Feeling his eyes bug, he cleared his throat and tried to speak.

"Oh my god, you hate it," she said, touching her hair. "I've always liked to dye it different colors. You know, artist and all?" Her lips formed a timid grin. "I hope you still want to bang me. Please say something—"

"You're beautiful," he blurted like a caveman who had just learned to speak instead of grunt. "Wow…" His eyes darted over her waist and the flare of her hips before lifting to her eyes, which popped underneath the liner and blue shadow. "I just… You're beautiful, Jus," he repeated, mentally kicking himself for being so lame.

Biting her lip, she studied him. "I *think* you're being truthful…"

Closing the distance between them, he snaked his arm around her waist and drew her close, pressing his lips to hers in a blazing kiss. His tongue dipped into her mouth, searching and tasting as she trembled in his arms. After thoroughly ravishing her, he broke the kiss, panting slightly as he gazed into her eyes. "I'm being truthful," he murmured.

"Whoa," she said, swaying as he held her firm. "I didn't know I needed to be kissed like that until you showed up tonight." Lifting her brows, she asked, "Did you bring the handcuffs?"

"Yes, woman," he said, pecking her lips. "I'm beginning to think you have a fetish."

"Obviously," she said, playfully rolling her eyes. "About time you figured it out."

Chuckling, he slid his hand into hers, leading her to the car and ensuring she was in safely before situating behind the wheel. They caught up on the day and made casual conversation as he drove to Battle Falls.

"I didn't even want to put this on," she said, lifting her light coat. "It's been so warm for late November, but, sadly, I think that's over."

"It's supposed to drop thirty degrees on Monday," he said, pulling into the restaurant and looking for a parking spot. "It was nice while it lasted."

Once parked, Gary walked around and opened her door, offering to carry her coat the short distance to the restaurant. She would need it later, and he checked it when they stepped inside before being led to their table.

Two small candles sat atop the white tablecloth in the dim restaurant, and he held her chair before lowering into his own. They ordered a bottle of red and enjoyed a glass before ordering an appetizer and their entrees. After they devoured the hummus and warm pita bread, Gary slid his hand over the table. Justine covered his palm with hers, holding tight as he asked her about her dreams. He wanted to know everything about her—what she craved, what made her tick, and what she wanted for the future.

"Well, I already mentioned I'd like to pop out another kid," she said, wrinkling her nose. "I think one is good because I'm pushing forty and can't imagine having the energy for more."

"Fair enough."

"And I want to continue to paint and sculpt. If things go well, I'd love to open my own gallery. It's a huge undertaking though, and so expensive. Avery's well-being is my first priority, so it would have to be well thought out."

"I'd invest in you, Jus, and I'm sure Peter could help you come up with some creative ways to finance the venture."

"Thank you, but you've got your own future to worry about since you're looking for a house. By the way, did you like the listing I sent you yesterday?" Anticipation swam in her eyes.

"I did," he said, grinning as he caressed her hand with his thumb. "It's in the same neighborhood your brother, Teresa, Carrie, and Peter live in."

"Yep," she said with a nod. "I figure the free babysitting is a bonus. You know, when you come and visit me in my house I'm going to buy."

"What if I buy it first?" he teased.

Her eyes narrowed. "You wouldn't."

Gary remained silent, arching his brows.

"Regardless, we definitely aren't buying it together." She was adorable as she gently chewed her lip. "I mean, that would be crazy...right?"

"Right," he said, his tone warm, indicating they were on the same page even if their words contradicted what they both wanted. In truth, the house was a three-bedroom modern style that was perfect if they decided to move in together, and they both knew it.

"So, I'm thinking about listing my home with Heather Combs. She recently got her real estate license, and I want to support a local female business owner."

Gary's eyes widened. "I've seen her a few times around town. Can't believe she had the guts to come back to Ardor Creek, especially since Butch married Cynthia."

"I think it says a lot about her fortitude. I know she was a bitch in high school and was terrible to Abby, and that blows, but maybe she's changed. I've spoken to her a few times since I saw her at my showing, and I kind of dig her."

"I guess everyone's capable of redemption," he said, leaning back as the server brought their entrees. "She never bothered me in school, but I know she was terrible to Abby."

"Maybe I can set up drinks with the three of us and Heather can apologize to her."

"Good luck with that," he muttered, taking a bite of steak.

"Hey! I think it's a great idea."

"I'm not sure Heather has any desire to apologize, but you could try."

"Maybe I will," she said with a firm nod.

"My woman, the peacemaker."

Squinting one eye, she said, "I'm not sure I'm down with being called your 'woman,'"—she made quotation marks with her fingers—"except it's kind of hot in a possessive sort of way."

"I didn't mean to offend you, hon. You know I'm possessive over you. Hell, I have no idea what you see in me half the time, but I'm glad you keep hanging around."

"I think *you* keep hanging around *me*," she teased.

"I sure do. Hope you never kick me out."

Rubbing her foot against his leg, she waggled her brows. "No way, buddy. You're stuck with me."

They finished their dinner as anticipation began to seethe between them. After dessert, Gary paid the bill and led her to the car, dying to ease the dress off her sexy body and make love to her. When they arrived home, he grabbed the handcuffs from the backseat, noticing the flash of arousal in Justine's eyes when they softly clanked.

After locking the door behind them, Justine hung her coat on the rack and headed toward the stairs.

"Not so fast, Ms. Lancaster," Gary called, encircling her wrist and drawing her toward him. "We don't let pretty little things like you off the hook so easily." Sliding one of the cuffs around her wrist, he clicked it into place.

"But Officer, I'm innocent." She pouted, brushing her breasts against his chest and driving him wild.

"I don't think so," he growled, latching onto her free wrist and twirling her. Aligning his cock with her luscious ass, he spoke softly in her ear. "We don't let bad girls free here." Locking the other cuff around her wrist, he tugged the chain that connected them, forcing her to slightly arch her back. Her pert breasts jutted, and he slid his palm over one as he held her immobile. "You'll need to be punished."

"Oh, god," she moaned, leaning her head on his shoulder. "Please punish me."

A sexy, almost sinister laugh escaped his throat. "You little tease." Resting his lips against the shell of her ear, he traced his finger over her nipple, which rapidly pebbled beneath the blue fabric. "You like being punished, don't you?"

"Yes," she rasped, squirming against him. "Please..."

Hooking his finger in the neckline of her dress, he tugged, drawing the dress down along with her bra. Her nipple stood firm in the dark foyer, and he pinched it as she hissed. "Do you want me to play with these pretty nipples while I punish you?"

"Yes," she breathed, rolling her head on his shoulder. "Fuck, this is so hot."

Gary pinched her nipple once more before bending down and lifting her into his arms. Once in her bedroom, he set her on her feet beside the bed. Lowering to one knee, he tugged off her heels. Rising, he gently turned her, feeling himself harden as she stood before him bound in his cuffs. Grasping the zipper of her dress, he dragged it down her back and pushed the fabric so it gathered at her waist. It bound her further, and Gary felt his eyes cross with lust.

"Do you know why I cuffed you, Ms. Lancaster?" he asked, unclasping her bra and shoving it toward her bunched dress.

"No," she whispered, shimmying against him.

"Because you looked at me with those fucking bedroom eyes all night," he murmured. Reaching around, he cupped her breasts and pulled her back into his front. "And I bet you were wet when we talked about me cuffing you, weren't you?" He plucked her nipples, causing her to moan before she nodded.

"Yes. I'm always wet around you. You're so hot—"

"Show me," he said, urging her toward the bed. Following his lead, she allowed him to guide her as her knees brushed the comforter. Once she was situated, he slowly urged her head toward the mattress. "Trust me, hon," he softly commanded.

Her muscles relaxed, and her trust set something free deep inside his soul. Before he'd lost the ability to perform, he and Nicole had been into light bondage play, and he'd always enjoyed it. There was something about controlling a sexual situation, especially when your partner showed ultimate trust. Since he'd always been a bit shy, he enjoyed the ability to show a more dominant side in the bedroom.

Justine wriggled on the bed as her cheek rested on the comforter. She looked like a bound angel, mussed and ready with her clothes bunched around her waist. Reaching for the hem of her dress, he pulled it high, over her bound wrists, and bared the gorgeous globes of her ass.

"Look at this naughty underwear," he said, sliding a finger under her thong and dragging it along her folds. She moaned against the bed, the sound so sexy in the dim room. Grabbing the thin scraps of her underwear, he slid her thong down her legs and tossed them aside. Placing his palms on the mounds of her ass, he spread her open, feeling the beast inside roar as he gazed at her deepest place.

"Mine," he growled, slowly running his thumbs over her wet folds. "Do you hear me, Justine?"

"Yours," she cried, pushing into his fingers. "Always."

He gave her ass a firm slap, elated when she whimpered with pleasure. "You're so greedy, Jus, pushing against me, begging me to slide my fingers inside you."

"Oh, god...please...inside me..."

Chuckling, he reached over and opened the drawer, pulling out the container of lube and unscrewing the cap. Setting the metal container on top of the dresser, he slathered his fingers in the smooth substance. Resting them against her pussy, he began to slowly trail them up and down along her swollen folds.

"Is it warm?" he asked.

"Yes. It feels so good."

Gary maneuvered his hands all over her sweet flesh, around the globes of her ass, and in every crevice of her trembling core.

Placing two fingers at her entrance, he surged inside, thrilled when her body bowed with pleasure.

He pumped inside her, adding a third finger when she pleaded for it, and Gary felt his cock growing hard and turgid inside his dress pants. Wanting to take advantage of the moment, he kicked off his shoes and unbuckled his belt, pushing his pants and underwear off before tearing away his shirt. Reaching for her, his fingers found her wet center again. Gliding to her clit, he began to stimulate it as he ran the head of his cock over her drenched core.

"I'm going to fuck you now, Jus," he said, the tone of his voice low and ragged. "Open that sweet pussy for me, honey."

"*Gary—*"

The word broke off as he impaled her, thrusting his cock inside her taut core. She grunted on the bed as he began to move, drawing his shaft through her wet folds before surging once again. Gliding his hands to her hips, he latched on, anchoring her as he began to fuck her in earnest.

"This is what bad girls get, honey," he gritted, overcome by the sound of their sweat-covered flesh slapping together. "They get fucked from behind. Do you like how I punish you?"

"Yes!" she wailed, thrusting her hips higher as he clutched them, begging him for more. "*Harder!*"

Too lost in her to get caught up in his normal worries, he slammed his body into hers, claiming her as she cried his name upon the bed. Leaning down, he pressed his lips against her ear as his hips hammered into hers.

"I can't give you up, Jus," he breathed in her ear. "This is all I ever wanted. Do you hear me?"

"I'm not going anywhere," she moaned, the sound laced with joyful amusement. "Not when you're balls-deep inside me...*ohhhh...fuck!* So good... Come in my pussy, Gary."

Heavy breaths rushed from his lungs as he felt his balls begin to tingle. Realizing he might actually finish inside her brought a burst of pleasure deep within. "I want you to come too—"

"Come inside me," she demanded. "I can come later. This is so hot...*oh, god...*"

"*Fuck...*" he growled, feeling his release form at the base of his cock. "I can't hold it back, hon..."

Her soft, sexy whimper shot straight to his dick, and he closed his eyes, feeling his shaft begin to jerk. Burying his face in her neck, he shot his release inside her tight channel, the soft walls milking him as he emptied everything inside her. His cock pulsed and shuddered before beginning to soften inside the sweet warmth. Moaning against her skin, he kissed her neck, wondering if she truly understood how long it had been since he'd crossed the chasm of climaxing during intercourse. Drawing back, he nudged her ear with his nose.

"Holy shit, Jus," he whispered.

"You fucked me good," she said, giggling. "Holy shit is right."

Gathering the strength to rise, he withdrew from her body, marveling at seeing her sweet essence glistening on his shaft. Reaching for his pants, he withdrew the handcuff key from his pocket and unlocked them. Setting them on the nightstand, he encircled her arms, helping her up. She pushed her bunched clothing to the floor before flopping back on the bed.

"Whew!" she exclaimed, swiping her forehead with her arm. "I did *not* expect that."

Crawling over her, he aligned their bodies and pressed his lips to hers. They gazed into each other's half-lidded eyes as they softly kissed.

"You're going to need to leave the handcuffs here. I'm sure the station can give you another pair."

Laughing, he nodded. "I can probably arrange that. I like a little bondage here and there."

"Um, yeah, I received that message loud and clear," she teased, biting her lip. "Maybe next time, you could cuff me to the bed and fuck me that way."

"I'm going to cuff you to the bed and kiss every part of your body, hon. I just need to recover first."

Trailing her fingers over his jaw, she smiled. "I'm game."

"Thank you for trusting me. It was so sweet to see you open up to me."

"No 'thank yous,'" she said, resting a finger over his lips. "Remember?"

Gently nipping her finger, he nodded. "I just haven't come like that in a long damn time."

"Well, I'm glad. We're so close to simultaneous orgasm. I've got the champagne ready for when we reach the pinnacle."

Resting his head on his hand, he studied her. "You can tell me if you ever get frustrated with our situation, Jus. You've been so understanding, but I want you to be honest with me."

"I don't think you understand how difficult sex was before you," she said, gently caressing his cheek. "This is the first safe, open sexual relationship I've had, Gary. I don't think you realize how special that is to me."

"I'm glad. I want you to feel safe with me."

"I do. Now, be a good boy and recover so we can go again."

Chuckling, he kissed the tip of her nose. "My bossy woman."

"Damn straight."

Reaching toward the handcuffs, his chest puffed with pleasure as her eyes lit with desire. Grasping the metal, he bound her to the headboard, ready to ravish her all over again.

Chapter 18

December arrived with a flurry of frigid weather and frenzied energy as Justine prepared for the Christmas holiday. She and Gary continued to spend time together as their relationship grew from an exciting spark to something true and deep. Each day spent with him reassured her that he was the man she wanted to spend her future with. Seeing his interactions with Avery also confirmed she wanted to have a child with him no matter the obstacles. Of course, first, they would need to decide to move in together, get engaged, and get married, but Justine had always had tunnel vision, and this situation was no different. Did it mean she moved too fast sometimes? Sure. But moving fast with Gary felt right, and they were both old enough to know what they wanted.

Deciding she would broach the subject with him, she relaxed into his side as they snuggled on her couch after Avery went to bed the Friday night before he was set to fly to Florida to see his parents for Christmas.

"I want this to be the last Christmas we spend apart, Gary," she said, gazing up at him as his arm rested across her shoulders.

His lips formed a soft smile. "Me too, hon."

Her eyes searched his as her heart pounded in anticipation of the serious discussion. "I want to talk to you about having kids. I know it's super-serious, but I don't have a ton of time left on the baby train."

Lifting the remote, he switched off the TV and shuffled to face her. "Okay, let's talk about it."

Gnawing her lip, she asked, "Okay, so your sperm count is compromised, right? Is that what the issue might be if we try?"

"Yes," he said with a nod. "A traumatic injury like mine affects sperm count. That, combined with my performance issues, makes it improbable we can conceive the old-fashioned way. Not impossible, but improbable, according to my doctors."

Digesting the information, she nodded. "Can we go see your doctor together? I'd like to talk about measures we can take if we can't conceive naturally. Like how long we should try before we begin other methods such as artificial insemination and IVF, if we have to go down that road. I mean, I'm no spring chicken myself. I could end up having issues too. Who the hell knows?"

Brown eyes caressed her features as he swiped a tuft of hair away from her forehead. "I'll be happy to go see the doc with you. It's a bit embarrassing, as this stuff always is, but I want to make you happy, Jus."

Justine noticed his slightly forlorn expression and ran her fingers over his jaw. "What's wrong? Am I freaking you out?"

Shaking his head, his gaze lowered. "I just wish I was normal. That you didn't have to deal with all this stuff with me. You know, the stuff in the bedroom and the extra work it will probably take to have a baby."

"Whoa," she said, placing her fingers under his chin to reclaim his gaze. "You're perfectly normal. Exceptional, actually. You make me so happy, Gary. I love our sexy times together. The way we communicate and how sweet you are when you put me first, which you do every damn time. That's so much more important to me than anything else. There are so many ways to make love, and I think we're pretty damn good at it." Biting her lip, she emitted a soft giggle.

"Sometimes, I wonder if you're going to wake up one day and realize you deserve better," he murmured, sadness in his deep brown eyes.

Tears stung her eyes at his forlorn expression. How did he not know how special he was to her? That she was so enamored with him she had no desire to even look at anyone else? Words pounded in her head as she contemplated saying them aloud. *I love you,*

Gary... The sentiment clanked in her brain as she debated telling him, knowing it would set them on the path to forever. Hell, she was ready for that with him, even though their relationship had only been romantic for a few months. Perhaps she should just blurt it out already.

"Gary, I—"

"Sorry," he said, shaking his head as he cracked a smile. "I don't want to make this about my injury. It's not conducive to dwell on something I can't change. I'm just happy you're so patient and caring with me, Jus. It's really something."

"You're pretty easy to care about, Gary," she said, scootching closer and nuzzling into his side. "I mean, if we're going to have a baby, we probably need to make this more serious. Are you ready to get married again?"

His throat bobbed as his eyes widened. "To you? In a damn heartbeat."

Chuckling, she kissed his chin. "Me too. To you. Or to Chris Evans. Whoever asks me first." Lifting her glass, she winked.

"Noted," he said, lifting his brows. "Seems like I've got some planning to do."

Wrinkling her nose, Justine couldn't stop the images of Dean's proposal from flashing through her mind.

"What is it?"

Sighing, she shrugged. "Dean proposed to me when we were at McDonald's." She huffed a breath. "He just looked at me over his hamburger and was like, '*We should get married so everybody knows you're off-limits, Justine. I'll buy you a ring next week at the jewelry store when they have their Independence Day sale.*'"

Gary grimaced. "Good lord. You're due for a really nice proposal then."

"Uh, yeah, I actually think I am. I aim to get one this time. You and Chris have a lot of work to do."

"Captain America has nothing on this guy," he said, pointing to his chest. "I'm going to propose the hell out of you, woman."

Justine couldn't contain her smile. "Promise?"

A long, slow breath exited his lungs as his gaze grew serious. "Yes. If that's what you want, hon."

Nodding, she tried to tamp down the tiny butterflies that were now fluttering in her chest. "It is," she whispered.

"Okay." Kissing the tip of her nose, he sat back and stroked her hair as he contemplated. "I'm on it. And I'll also call my doctor and see what appointments he has available for January."

"Thank you. I know it's not an easy subject, but I appreciate you being open with me."

His fingers slowly caressed her hair. "I figured the window to have kids was closed for me," he murmured. "I never dreamed I'd be talking about having one with you."

"*Two* with me," she corrected, lifting her finger. "Avery loves you so much, and we'll cross that bridge once we tackle all this other serious stuff. Peter officially adopted Carrie's boys once they got married, and I'd want you to do the same with Avery."

"I'd be honored. I love her like my own daughter."

"I know," Justine whispered, overcome with how lucky she and Avery were to have him. "Your bond is so special. Sometimes, I'm a bit jealous, to be honest." She held her thumb and forefinger an inch apart as she squinted.

Chuckling, he squeezed her shoulder. "We'll remember to include you...most of the time."

"Jerk," she chided, slapping his shoulder. "Okay, I think you've earned the right to turn whatever sports event you were watching before I dragged you into this awkward serious discussion back on."

Flashing a grin, he lifted the remote and turned on the TV. The commentators' voices chimed in the background as they relaxed on the couch. Relieved at the fruitful discussion, Justine sipped her wine as her mind drifted to the future, imagining all the things they would hopefully create together.

Chapter 19

G ary had a nice holiday with his parents in Florida. He'd already told them his relationship with Justine had turned romantic, and his mother could barely contain her excitement when he informed her he was going to propose.

"Oh, that's wonderful, Gary," his mom said as they sat on their screened-in back porch. They lived in a senior community comprised of spacious modern houses around a large lake built in the center. "Does this mean you're going to give me some grandbabies? I'd given up hope."

"Good lord, Melissa," his father said, holding the newspaper high as he half-listened to the conversation. "Let the man propose before you jump eight steps ahead."

"It's a perfectly normal question, Bill," Melissa chimed, shooting him a glare. "And I would like an answer please."

"We're going to try, Mom," Gary said, foot waggling atop his knee as he relaxed in the chair. "She's already got Avery, and she's a sweetheart. I've promised them we'll visit you next year and take her to Disney World."

"Oh, this is so special." Melissa held her palms to her cheeks. "We need to buy a new pull-out couch, Bill. The one we have is broken, and we'll need a place for Gary's new crew to stay."

"One thing at a time, Mom," he said, holding up a hand. "The second bedroom is fine for now, and I'll send money for a new pull-out couch in the den once we get there. Let me get her to say yes first."

Reaching over, his mother grabbed his hand, squeezing so hard Gary thought he might lose circulation. "After everything that happened with your *ex-wife*,"—she rolled her eyes—"I'm just so happy you found a lovely, kind woman this time."

Melissa had never taken to Nicole, which had always disappointed Gary. He knew deep in his heart she would love Justine and Avery as much as he did. Knowing his mother was biased since she loved him, he felt the need to defend Nicole.

"It takes two people to make a marriage work, Mom. I don't blame Nicole, and you shouldn't either."

Sitting back, she crossed her arms and gave a "*harrumph.*" "You and your father have this forgiveness streak I'll never understand. That woman was a B with an itch, if you know what I mean."

"You can say 'bitch,' sweetheart," Bill muttered, turning the page of his newspaper. "And they were too young to get married. It was doomed from the start."

"Love the positivity, Dad," Gary teased, rising and patting his shoulder. "Thanks. I'm going to grab a beer now that it's officially noon. That's what you all do in Florida on Christmas holiday, right?"

"Every day's a holiday when you're retired, dear," Melissa said, rising and falling into step beside him as they walked into the kitchen. "Two more days until Christmas and I'm glad to have every second with you before you fly home. I'm glad you were able to get time off to visit."

"Me too. I intend on making it a priority because I want you to know the girls, Mom. They're so special."

Melissa's eyes sparkled as she patted his cheek. "My baby's in love. I think I'll have some rosé with you. What a happy day."

Smiling, Gary joined his mother in a toast while chuckling at the fact she poured half the bottle into her rather large wineglass.

On Christmas Eve morning, Justine was at her wit's end. She woke up to a sick, crying daughter who was violently puking on every inch of her pink princess sheets. After giving her a bath where Justine plucked gross chunks out of Avery's hair, she called the pediatrician, worried she might need to take her to the hospital.

"There's a twenty-four-hour bug going around, Justine," Dr. Mc-Sweeny's deep voice said on the other end of the phone. "You can take her to the ER, but you're the fifth call I've received this morning. Avery likely picked it up at school, and it should pass by tomorrow."

"Okay," Justine said, worried as she stroked Avery's now-damp hair. "What should I do to help her?"

"Children's Tylenol to start, and ice cream if she can get something down. I've learned that ice cream always helps the children and the parents since it's universally loved. You can also give her Sprite or ginger ale if you want to try and settle her stomach."

"Will do. Thanks, doc."

Since Avery's bed was still barf-covered, Justine gave her some Children's Tylenol and placed her in her bed, hoping she wouldn't make a mess there too. She lay with her until she fell asleep before assessing Avery's sheets and comforter. Deciding she'd rather buy new ones than deal with the stains, she gathered them into a large ball and headed out the front door to stuff them in the garbage can that sat in her driveway.

"Are you stuffing a body in there?" Jeremy's voice called from his driveway. "You look mad as a hornet. Do I need to add this scene to my novel?"

Covering the garbage with the plastic top, she turned and swiped her forehead. "Barf emergency. Avery has a stomach bug that seems to be plaguing Ardor Creek public schools. Are your girls affected?"

"Both sick as dogs," he said, nodding. "We were going to go visit Jenny tonight and open presents together with her new boyfriend, but she wanted to save him the grief." He grimaced. "I think she really likes this guy, and puking kids aren't sexy."

"They sure aren't." Justine's breath fogged in the cold as she spoke. "It's a bummer for Christmas Eve, huh? I already called my parents and told them we're not coming. I don't want to get anyone sick, and honestly, I don't think I can handle cleaning up my car too. Better safe than sorry."

"Truth. I'm grabbing some more logs for the fireplace, and they're both passed out on the couch."

"Same here. Hey, if the kids start to feel better, we should open presents by my tree. It's not the same as doing it with the whole family, but it will give them something to celebrate."

"The girls would love that. I'll text you if they start to feel better, and you do the same. Sending some good vibes to Avery."

"Thanks," she said, waving before walking through the front door. "Hope your girls feel better too."

Justine placed fresh sheets on Avery's bed and tinkered in the kitchen until she called her name. Jogging up the stairs, she found Avery sitting up and was pleased some of the color had returned to her cheeks.

"How you feeling, baby?" she asked, sitting on the side of the bed and stroking her cheek.

"My tummy still hurts, Mommy," she said, her lips forming a slight pout. "I want ice cream."

Breathing a laugh, Justine tilted her head. "If your tummy hurt that bad, you probably wouldn't want any ice cream."

"It doesn't hurt as bad as before," she said, flashing an adorably mischievous grin that sent a jolt of relief through Justine. Knowing her daughter was on the way to recovery, she leaned over and gathered her in her arms. "Okay, we'll have one scoop, and I want you to have some Sprite too. It will help settle your stomach."

"Thanks, Mom."

"You're welcome."

Once they were in the kitchen, Justine prepared the ice cream and soda before sitting beside Avery at the table. "Jeremy's girls are sick too," she said, resting her chin on her hand as Avery slowly ate the ice cream. "If they begin to feel better like you are, we'll have them over to open presents with us since we're not going to Grandma and Grandpa's."

Avery nodded, and Justine sat with her for a few more minutes before plopping her on the couch to rest as she watched Christmas cartoons. Around five o'clock, her phone rang, and she lifted it to her ear.

"Next door neighbor and thriller protagonist here," she teased into the phone. "Who's calling?"

Jeremy chuckled. "I can't wait for you to read this manuscript. You're giving me such good stuff, Justine. Anyway, the girls are feeling well enough to open presents. Is the offer to come over still open? I think it would be nice for the kids to do it together if Avery is up to it."

"She's feeling much better too. Come on over. I made chocolate chip cookies and chili today. That's the extent of my Christmas cooking, so if you want something else, bring it over."

"That's perfect. We'll only stay for a bit. I want to get them to bed early."

They arrived fifteen minutes later, Jeremy carrying a bag of presents that he placed under Justine's tree. The girls opened their gifts together as she and Jeremy took videos, and Justine's mind wandered to Gary, excited to show him the videos of Avery opening his present. He'd gotten her a stuffed Minnie Mouse plushy doll to cuddle with, and it was the precursor to them telling her they were going to take her to Disney World next year.

Eventually, all the presents were opened, and Justine could tell the girls were getting tired. Jeremy wrangled up his twins, Angeline and Gabby, and shuffled them to the front door. Justine tugged it open, and the girls trailed outside, walking toward their house. Jeremy stood in the doorway, and Justine crossed her arms to ward off the chill.

"That was fun," she said, smiling up at him. "At least the entire holiday wasn't ruined."

"Seriously. Thanks for having us over." He hesitated as his light green eyes darted over her face. "Can I, uh, ask you something?"

"Sure."

"I know you're dating the cop and he's a really nice guy. I've also learned that you miss a hundred percent of the shots you never take."

"Gary would appreciate that sports analogy," Justine said, chuckling.

Jeremy grinned. "The thing is, Justine, I like you. A lot. Our kids get along well, and I wouldn't forgive myself if I didn't ask you on a date. I have no idea how serious it is with Gary, but if you all aren't exclusive, I'd love to take you out."

Justine was flattered at the offer, although it was too late. Gary already owned every piece of her heart, and she hoped he never gave it back. Wanting to be kind, she cupped his arm. "That's so sweet, Jeremy, and a few months ago, I would've jumped on it."

"Damn. I should've asked you out that first day you scared the crap out of me in front of my house."

Laughing, she lifted a shoulder. "Maybe, but the thing is, I think I've been in love with Gary for a while. I didn't have the best experience with love the first time around, so I don't think I realized it when it happened again. It's a much different experience this time, and I'm not going to be dumb enough to fuck it up again."

"I'm so happy to hear that, Justine. It gives me hope for my next time around too."

"You're so kind and thoughtful, and a best-selling author to boot. Any woman is going to be lucky to snag you."

"And exceedingly handsome, right?" he pointed at his face. "My ego needs the affirmation after your excruciating rejection."

"Okay, dramatic author," she said, playfully shoving him out the door. "That was a perfectly nice, calm rejection, thank you very much." Turning on the doorstep, he leaned in to hug her before drawing back. "And you're easy on the eyes, if that makes you feel better."

He playfully bowed and circled his hand in mock reverence. "Thank you. My ego is restored."

"If I were trying to matchmake, I'd inform you that Heather Combs certainly seemed to have her eye on you at my showing when you two met." She waggled her eyebrows.

Jeremy's eyes grew wide as he blew a breath from puffed cheeks. "She seems like...a lot."

"Well, that might be fun. Who knows?"

"Fun," he murmured, rubbing his chin. "Haven't tried that in a while. I'll keep it in mind."

"Merry Christmas, Jeremy," she said, leaning on the door as she grinned. "I'm glad we're friends."

"Me too. See you later." Giving a wave, he trailed across the yard toward his home.

"I'm going to sleep with Minnie tonight," Avery said, tugging Justine's sweater as she closed the door. "Will you take a picture and send it to Gary?"

"I sure will," she said, bending down and running a hand over her hair. "Let's get your teeth brushed and maybe we can video chat with him while I read *'Twas the Night Before Christmas* to you. Sound good?"

Avery gave a fervent nod before jogging up the stairs. "Bribery for time with Gary works every damn time, Jus." Patting herself on the back, she headed to clean up the wrapping paper in the living room. "You've got this mom thing figured out."

Snickering to herself, she cleaned up and tucked Avery into bed before they called Gary. As they video chatted, joy welled in Justine's heart at the fact they'd all be together next Christmas. And maybe they'd even be married with another child on the way. Reminding herself to take a chill pill, she relaxed into Avery's mattress as her baby cuddled against her while she read.

Chapter 20

The day after Christmas, Gary hugged his parents goodbye and headed home. On the plane, he rewatched the videos Justine had sent him of Avery opening her presents. She was adorable when she opened the stuffed Minnie Mouse he'd gotten her...as she sat beside Jeremy's daughters. Frowning, Gary realized something rubbed him the wrong way about Jeremy spending Christmas Eve with his girls while he was away. He understood it was a last-minute change due to the stomach bug, but it bothered him nonetheless. Chalking it up to the slightly possessive streak he exhibited with Justine, he told himself to relax and let it go.

When he got home, he drove straight to Justine's house, acknowledging the visceral need to see her and Avery. After parking in the driveway and exiting his car, he grinned as Avery bounded from the front door and ran to him through the snow.

"Thank you for my stuffed Minnie, Gary," she said, holding up the doll as she jogged toward him. Gary opened his arms and lifted her, grinning as he hugged her before situating her on his hip.

"You're welcome. I'm so glad you like it, Ave."

"I missed you," she said, kissing his cheek.

Love swelled as he tugged a strand of her hair. "I missed you too, sweetheart."

He carried her toward the door where Justine was waiting, gorgeous as anticipation swelled in her eyes. "Hey, stranger. About time you got home."

"Hey, hon." Setting Avery on the wooden floor of the foyer, he watched her scamper away as he drew Justine close. "I missed you so damn much." Cupping her ass with one hand, he thrust the other into her short hair and pulled her into a blazing kiss.

After he'd thoroughly devoured her lips, she drew back and gave a wistful sigh. "Five hours and fourteen minutes until bedtime." Lifting her wrist, she shook it as her watch gleamed. "Not that I'm counting the hours until I can bang you or anything."

Grinning, he rested his forehead on hers. "I'm counting the fucking seconds, honey. I can't wait to touch you."

They settled in the living room, Avery playing with some of her new presents on the carpeted floor as Justine and Gary caught up while they relaxed on the couch.

"My parents are on board for Disney World. They're dying for us to stay with them."

"I can't wait," she said, resting her head on the back of the couch. "I remember meeting them around town, but it will be nice to get to know them better."

"They feel the same way." Taking her hand, he caressed the silken skin with his thumb. "Can I give you my present now?"

They'd decided to wait to exchange gifts until he returned. Gary had mentioned he'd gotten something for her and was elated when she gave him a shy smile and informed him she'd gotten him a present as well.

"Definitely. I've got to grab mine in the bedroom. One sec." Rising from the couch, she trailed up the steps. Gary headed outside and grabbed her present from the car. Once they were both seated again, she tentatively extended a long, thin wrapped box, grinning as she bit her lip. "I hope it's not dumb. There's this place in the mall, and I had to make them for you. Well, for us, really."

"Them?" he asked, curious. Ripping away the paper, he opened the box to reveal three t-shirts. The largest one read "#1 Steelers Fan," and the medium-size one read "Steelers Fan Because of This Guy" and pictured a hand with a finger pointing to the side. The smallest one read, "#1 Steelers Fan's Biggest Fan."

Unable to control his grin, he held them up. "These are awesome, Jus."

"Yeah, I figured we could wear them when you watch football and Avery and I pretend to like it."

Tossing back his head, he laughed before leaning in to kiss her. "They're perfect. Thank you, honey."

"You're welcome."

After folding the shirts back in the box, he reached for her gift and handed it to her. Justine unwrapped it and pulled out the frame, examining it.

"It's a 'first dollar earned' frame with an engravable plaque. You put the first dollar you earn at your gallery there," he said, pointing, "your business card there, and then we can engrave your gallery name and date on the plaque when it happens."

Her chin wobbled as she gently turned the frame in her hands.

"Don't cry, hon," he said, sliding his fingers under her chin. "I believe in you and know you can do it. This was supposed to make you smile."

Shaking her head, she swiped away an errant tear. "It's amazing. It took years for my parents to support my career as an artist, but I mention one time to you that I want to open a gallery, and you buy me this." Lifting the frame, she warbled a laugh. "You're so supportive, Gary. I appreciate you so much."

"I*m* supportive?" he asked, sliding across the couch and drawing her into his arms. "Hell, Jus, you're the representation of the damn word." Placing a soft kiss on her lips, he stared deeply into her eyes. "You're so patient with my issues. I want to do my part to support you half as much as you support me."

"You don't have any issues," she said, gently rolling her eyes. "But this is lovely. Thank you, Gary. I can't wait to engrave it."

"Me either."

Avery interrupted them, asking if she could have a juice box, which effectively ended the moment. Sparing each other one last tender glance, they headed to the kitchen to scrounge up a juice box and a snack for their little girl.

Gary returned to work as the short, cold days of January settled in. He'd picked up some extra shifts to secure the days off when he visited his parents, which meant he saw less of his girls than he wanted. When he did steal time with them, it was never enough, and Gary realized it was time to look for a ring and plan his proposal.

Yes, he and Justine had only technically been dating for a few months, but they'd had some pretty serious discussions and shared a vision for the future. Gary craved having a child with her and figured sooner rather than later was best since he wasn't getting any younger. He loved her and Avery with his entire heart and would do everything in his power to make them happy.

Gary scheduled two appointments with a reproductive endocrinologist who specialized in male and female fertility. The physician he'd used after his injury had since moved to North Carolina but had highly recommended Dr. Nancy Spenser. For the first appointment, he went in for routine blood work and gave a sperm sample, and Dr. Spenser inspected his injured pelvic region. It was highly uncomfortable for Gary, but Dr. Spenser was a nice, genial woman who did her best to put him at ease.

"These appointments are never comfortable," she said as he sat on the exam table covered in the cloth gown. "I'm going to run my gloved hands over your private parts and squish them around while I ask questions." She held up her hands, covered in blue gloves as she rotated them. "You can tell me anything and everything you're feeling, and if you want to stop, we will. Ready?"

Her features were set in an expression that relayed her confidence under her brown, functional bun, glasses, and green irises.

"Ready."

He lay back on the table. and she examined his injured area, asking questions along the way. Eventually, he dressed, and she asked him to return in a week for a follow-up appointment where they would discuss the results with Justine.

One week later, as Justine sat in the waiting room beside him, she whispered, "Should I be mad this lady touched you in places that no one should see but me?"

Breathing a laugh, he eyed the receptionist behind the window, hoping she couldn't hear their discussion. "She didn't do it for me, Jus. I have a thing for blue-haired artists who like handcuffs. Go figure."

"Noted," she said, waggling her brows.

The nurse appeared and called them to Dr. Spenser's office, directing them to sit in the plushy leather chairs in front of her desk. Moments later, she strode in, tablet in hand, and sat behind the desk.

"Hello, Gary. Nice to see you again. And you must be Justine."

"Nice to meet you, Dr. Spenser."

"Nancy is fine if you prefer that. After all, we need to be comfortable for this discussion, right?"

"I'm not sure 'comfortable' is the right word, but, sure, let's go with that," Justine said, making quotation marks with her fingers.

Smiling, Dr. Spenser clicked the tablet with her stylus. "I'm just pulling up your results, Gary. I looked them over this morning, and we have some options to discuss."

Feeling his mood deflate, he shifted in his chair. "So, it's bad?"

"'Bad' and 'good' don't really apply in these situations," she said with a slight shrug. "You suffered a traumatic injury that reduced your sperm count, and we're here to assess your options. After looking at your results, your sperm count is just above the level we like to see to conceive naturally."

"Meaning what?" he asked.

"Meaning that you can try for a while the old-fashioned way and see if you conceive. You work out and are healthy, so that's a good start. If the traditional way doesn't work after a few months, I would suggest trying assisted reproduction."

"Like IVF?" Justine asked.

"IVF is the second option I would try because it's expensive and sometimes not covered by insurance. The first method I would suggest is intrauterine insemination, or IUI for short. This procedure involves Justine taking a drug called clomiphene to support egg development. At the time of ovulation, Gary supplies sperm in a cup that's then washed and concentrated. Next, the sperm is placed in the uterus using a long, flexible tube."

Justine took out her phone, jotting down notes as the doctor spoke. Gary watched her, feeling the old anger and embarrassment well inside at the thought of putting her through the extra procedure.

"If that fails, then we would try IVF," Dr. Spenser continued. Sitting back in her chair, she observed them. "It's a lot to take in, so if you'd like, I can give you some time to discuss, and I'm always available to meet with you again or do a Zoom appointment."

"It seems pretty straightforward to me," Justine said, glancing at Gary. "Guess this means I'm stopping the pill."

"Yes, that is a key requirement to conceiving the old-fashioned way," Dr. Spencer teased as amusement glowed in her eyes.

They chatted for a few more minutes before shaking the kind doctor's hand and exiting the office. Once in the car, Justine turned her head on the seat rest and grinned as he drove.

"Well, that was intense."

Gary's lips fluttered as he heaved out a breath. "Sure was. I'm so sorry about all the unknowns, Jus. It's really frustrating."

"Do I look frustrated?" she asked, pointing at herself. "I'm all good, here, Gary. I'm fine going off the pill, but I kind of want to be sure you're going to marry me if you knock me up."

Reaching over, he grabbed her hand before lifting it to his lips. "I'm working on it, honey. I want to make it special for you. My work schedule has been crazy. It will calm down a bit in February."

"I guess I'm fine with coming in second to protecting the citizens of Ardor Creek."

"No way," he said, nipping her fingers. "You and Avery are always first."

She smiled, silently acknowledging his statement.

The next day, Gary called Heather Combs after finding her number online. When she answered, he cleared his throat, trying to recall the last time he'd actually spoken to her.

"Hey, Heather, it's Gary Lincoln. Found your number online. I didn't realize you were working at Chandler Grossman's real estate firm."

"Hey, Gary. Sure am. The old geezer is going to retire soon, and he's sponsoring my real estate license. After I make fifty sales, I'm going to apply for my own brokerage license and hope to take over his firm once he retires and moves to whatever fair-weather state he chooses."

Chuckling at her brashness, he nodded as he sat behind the wheel of his police cruiser. "He's been the main real estate broker in town for decades. Good plan."

"Don't I know it. And it allows me to show the two condos for sale next to Butch and Cynthia's to every disreputable buyer in town. If you know anyone on meth, send them my way. They're perfect candidates to move in next to my ex-husband and his trash heap of a wife."

"Well, don't hold back, Heather. And you do realize I'm a cop, right? Anyone I know who has meth will be promptly arrested."

"*Ohh*, arrest them *at* the condo next to Butch's," she chimed, elation in her voice. "It will decimate his property value. My wheels are churning. Anyway, what's up?"

"I'd like to take a look at the house in the development on Cyprus Street. The last one that hasn't been sold."

"Yep, I know the one. I won't make a flippant comment about how you're getting the band back together since Peter and Mark live in that development."

Gary's eyebrows drew together. "I think you just did."

A laugh echoed over the phone. "True. I've always been too sarcastic for my own good. I can show you the house. My fee is four percent if you buy it, but I'll do it for three percent since I was such a bitch in high school. Having Officer Lincoln as a happy client would do wonders for my business."

Gary pondered as he remembered the discussion he'd had with Justine. "Actually, Justine is a fan of yours—maybe because she was younger than us."

"Or because I'm awesome, but go on..."

Huffing a laugh, he continued. "She wants to put together a happy hour or brunch with you and Abby so you can bury the hatchet."

"Ew. You're back to four percent, buddy."

"Come on, Heather. Three percent, brunch with Justine and Abby, and you're hired."

A forceful groan rang over the phone. "Fine. But you'd better give me a glowing review, Gary. I'm talking Yelp, Google, and every other search engine I can think of."

"You got it. Now, let me tell you what I'm thinking. I want to see the house, and if I like it, I have a whole thing planned..."

After detailing his plans, he could sense Heather's approval. "Justine's a lucky woman. I'm happy for you, Gary."

"Thanks. I'm proud of you for coming back to Ardor Creek, Heather. It couldn't have been easy after your divorce and some of the more colorful ancient history."

"Like the fact the mayor hates me?" she chided. "I deserve it, but I'm not going to sit and cry over things I can't change. There was a narrative about me in this town that had already been written, and a new one my shithead ex was trying to write, and I decided to take control of my own damn story."

"Good for you. I'm excited to see you when you schedule the showing. Text me your number and I'll text you Justine's. Give her a call so you all can set the brunch, okay?"

"10-4, Officer. See ya."

Wanting to tell Justine about his conversation regarding Abby while leaving the other parts a secret, he drove over in his cruiser and parked in front of her house. Using the key she'd given him, he walked inside to find her bent over the dishwasher with Jeremy Kramer's body wrapped over hers. Physically denying the urge to grab his shirt and rip him away, he loudly cleared his throat.

They both started before slowly untangling and rising. Giving him a huge grin, she stepped forward and lifted to her toes to kiss him. "My dishwasher's on the fritz, and I can't get this damn part to click," she said, holding up the piece. "I called Jeremy over and we tried to jam it in together, but it wouldn't work. Want to try?"

The thought of Jeremy jamming anything where Justine was concerned caused rage to well within. She'd mentioned he had asked her out over Christmas, and he wanted to pull the guy aside and tell him in no uncertain terms she was *his*. Of course, that was sexist as hell and not appropriate in civilized society, so he took the piece and headed toward the dishwasher. Pulling the flashlight from his duty belt, he examined the dim space. Gary was pretty handy and immediately saw the indention where the piece needed to be secured. Aligning it, he toyed around for several seconds before popping it into place.

"Well, I've been shown up," Jeremy said, showing his palms. "I tried to tell you I wasn't handy, Justine."

"Next time, just call me," Gary said, rising and reaching for the towel on the counter. Wiping his hands, he threw it aside and crossed his arms over his chest. "If I'm not involved in an arrest, I can always cruise by."

"Well, my damage here is done. I've got another chapter to finish before I go get the girls at school. Justine is very serious about the carpool schedule," he said, giving her an affectionate grin that made Gary want to rip the man's lips off. "See you guys later." He trailed out the back door, and Justine flashed a smile.

"Thanks for saving the day."

"You're welcome."

Sliding her arms around his neck, she tilted her head, assessing him. "Are you mad I asked Jeremy to help me instead of you?"

Narrowing his eyes, he muttered, "No."

Her lips pursed as she visibly held in a laugh.

"It's not funny, Justine. You told me he asked you out. I don't like him."

"I *told* you that I promptly said 'no' because I'm crazy about *you*. And I want to set him up with Heather. For some crazy reason, I think they would work."

He squinted. "I don't know. She might eat him alive. He's kind of a pussy."

Tossing back her head, she laughed. "He absolutely is not. Now, do me a favor and tell me why you're here."

"Actually, I wanted to tell you about Heather. I ran into her in town today," he said, using the white lie to cover up his secret plan. "She agreed to happy hour or brunch with you and Abby to bury the hatchet. She's going to reach out to you."

"Yay! I can't wait. Thank you for setting it up." Stealing a kiss, she shook her head. "And you know I only have eyes for you, right? Jeremy is my friend, Gary. I really like him, and I want you to get to know him. He's a cool dude."

His eyes darted between hers as he searched her eyes. "It would probably be easier if you chose someone like him. You wouldn't need the doctor's appointments and the extreme patience in the bedroom—"

"Whoa," she said, covering his lips. "You're not serious, are you? Please tell me you're not serious. We've been over this, Gary. I don't mind any of that as long as I have you. It hurts that you doubt me on that."

"I don't doubt you," he said softly. "I doubt myself because it presents extra challenges you wouldn't have with someone else."

Glancing toward the ceiling, her jaw clenched before she reclaimed his gaze. "I need you to trust that it doesn't bother me, Gary. Please. I don't want this to become an issue when it's not. I'm not Nicole."

Sighing, he nodded, realizing they were on the edge of getting into a fight, which was the last thing he wanted. "Okay, hon."

Drawing back, her eyes raked over him in his uniform. "Also, you look really hot right now. Why have we never banged when you're wearing your uniform? We're going to have to remedy that on Sunday. Remember, my parents are keeping Avery after Sunday dinner so we can have some alone time." She waggled her brows.

"I'll have the uniform pressed and ready," he teased, kissing her forehead. His walkie-talkie crackled with a call from the station, and he lifted it, listening to the voice report a disturbance at the abandoned warehouse on the outskirts of town. "10-4," he said into the device. "Officer Lincoln here. I'll head to the site and check it out. I'm on Maple Street and can be there in ten minutes."

"You're not at that pretty lady's house on Maple Street during duty, are you, Officer Lincoln?" the dispatcher asked.

"Mind your business, Jerry," he said into the receiver. "I'll report back in ten."

"Small towns," Justine said, rolling her eyes. "Gotta love 'em. Go save the day."

After one last peck on her soft lips, Gary rolled out to answer the call.

Chapter 21

Heather called Justine a few days later, and Justine planned brunch for them on the following Saturday. Gary offered to stay at home with Avery, which elated her daughter.

"Be good for Gary and don't scare him away," she teased, chucking Avery on the nose as she bent down to give her a hug in the foyer. "We want to keep him."

"We're going to play with the dollhouse. He says he can get the lights to work."

Rising, Justine smiled at Gary. "I plug the darn thing into the wall, but the lights stopped working years ago."

"It's probably a short. I think I can fix it. You must have a fancy dollhouse for it to light up," Gary said to Avery.

Beaming, she gave a ferocious nod.

"You two have fun. Bye!" Waving, she closed the door behind her, excited to have an adult brunch and a mimosa or two. Once she arrived at the restaurant, she headed inside and saw Abby sitting at a table in the back corner. The hostess led her over, and Justine slung her coat over the back of her seat.

"You're early."

"I'm nervous," Abby said, biting her lip. "How dumb is that? The crap with Heather happened twenty years ago, for Christ's sake."

"I wasn't around for the torture, but Carrie and Mark have told me she was awful to you. That really blows, but she's been nothing but cool with me. I like her and honestly feel a bit sorry for her. She moved back to a town where a lot of people dislike her, her ex-husband is remarried, and she's trying to build a business. It's got to be hard."

"I'm a huge supporter of female-owned businesses in Ardor Creek and want her to succeed. Even with our past issues, I would be happy to help her."

"I think being a friend to her would help even more. I want to invite her to hang with us because you all have been so amazing including me in the group, but I felt it would be awkward if you didn't talk first."

Abby nodded, swiping her brown hair off her shoulder. "Truth. I'm glad you set this up. Aaaaaand she's walking toward us. The chunky teenage girl in me wants to melt into the chair."

"You've got this," Justine said, squeezing her hand.

"Hi, ladies," Heather said, giving an absent wave as she tugged off her coat and rested it on the back of her chair. Fluffing her perfect hair, she sat and picked up the laminated brunch menu. "Do I need to order booze before we go any further?"

Laughing, they nodded. "I think booze is always called for," Justine said as the waitress walked over. They decided to order a mimosa pitcher and three glasses. Once the champagne flutes were full, they lifted them to toast.

"To putting the past behind us. I'm happy to have you throw that one in my face if it will make you feel better, Abby."

Grinning, Abby clinked her glass against Heather's and then Justine's. "Wouldn't that give Ardor Creek something to gossip about?" Lifting her brows, she sipped the mimosa.

"Seriously," Heather muttered before drinking. Once they'd placed their food order, they sat back and made small talk before Justine ushered along the main conversation.

"The reason why I wanted to get together is that I consider you both friends. I went through a period in my life during my marriage where I felt very alone. After my divorce, Abby and her friends brought me into their group and reminded me how awesome it was to have true friendship. It would be so fun if we could hang out together and start fresh."

"I'm happy to," Abby said with a nod. "High school was ages ago. I can put it behind me if you can."

Heather stroked the stem of her glass as she contemplated. "I can, but I need to apologize to you first, Abby. A *real* apology. But I'm not going to grovel because I also had hard times in high school and did the best I could."

Justine remembered Mark and Gary mentioning Heather's parents had been absent and possibly abusive. Reaching over, she squeezed her wrist. "We all make mistakes, especially when we're young."

"We do," she said, tilting her head. "I was a huge bitch because I was the prettiest girl in school and it gave me something to latch onto when I felt dead and empty inside. You were an easy target, Abby, because you were so shy and awkward."

Clearing her throat, Abby muttered, "I'm still waiting for the apology."

Heather breathed a laugh. "It's coming. Stay tuned." Lifting her glass, she chugged the rest of her mimosa before pouring another from the pitcher. "I always thought Chad had a thing for you even if he didn't realize it. He was always so nice to you, and it pissed me off. If smart, quirky girls like you could get a guy like Chad, it left no value for girls like me who had one quality: being pretty."

"I'm sorry you felt that way," Abby said, shaking her head. "As we all remember, Chad pretty much ruined any chance I had of fitting in senior year."

"You always blamed Chad, but it was really Butch's fault. You didn't know this, but I was really pissed at him for starting the chant. Yes, I joined in because I was a dumb teenager and needed to keep up my 'cool' appearance,"—she made quotation marks with her fingers—"but I cursed him out that night. I reminded him my father got off on hurting people and making them feel like shit, and I didn't want to be with someone who did the same. I didn't bone him for a month afterward, if that makes you feel better. It really pissed him off." Taking a sip, she gave a cheeky smile. "Bastard."

"Well, okay then," Abby said, awkwardly rubbing the back of her neck. "That might be TMI, but I'm glad he suffered a little. I think I blamed Chad more than Butch because he pretended to be my friend and then hurt me terribly. Butch never did anything but make fun of me."

"Chad wasn't pretending, Abby," Heather said softly. "I mean, he fell all over himself to marry you all these years later. He was probably in love with you then and just made a dumb mistake."

"He says the same thing," Abby said with a wistful sigh. "He swears he had a crush on me, which I find so hard to believe. But now we have Zoey and he's the best freaking husband, so I kind of forgive him." She playfully rolled her eyes.

"Well, anyway, I'm sorry. I can't change it, but I'd really like to try and be friends. Justine is right that I don't have a lot of them here, and I'm probably too brash for the locals. I need strong women who get me and can knock me off my high horse if I get too full of myself. Your crew is the strongest bunch of bitches in town, so I'd really like to hang if you can handle me."

"Apology accepted," Abby said, "and I'd love to hang. Carrie and Ashlyn were so sweet to me when I moved back, and I know how hard it is."

"Seriously," Heather said, leaning back in her chair as she held the mimosa. "How in the hell do people get laid in this town? There is a severe lack of eligible bachelors."

"Smitty doesn't do it for you?" Justine teased.

"I'm almost at the point where I'm going to climb him like a tree. Do you think he carries Viagra in his pocket, or should I get some samples from Dr. Matthews?"

Justine almost spit out her drink. "Hell, he might be great in bed. I hear he's dating Edna Schultz, but who knows?"

"Good lord, I can't even snag Smitty. Might as well throw some concrete between my thighs and let it set."

"You know, I've become pretty good friends with Jeremy," Justine said, her tone mischievous as she drew out his name. "He's really sweet and very cute."

"Yeah, he's on my list," Heather said as the server set their plates in front of them. Digging into her French toast, she shrugged. "I'm not really down with the kids thing though. It's one of many reasons Butch and I didn't make it."

"I didn't realize," Justine said, feeling her lips purse. "He wanted them and you didn't?"

"Yep," Heather said, dousing her meal with syrup. "I always knew I'd never be any good with kids. I had zero foundation for that. Butch and I probably should've talked about that before we got married, huh? Guess you don't think about that stuff when you get married right out of high school."

"So, you wouldn't consider dating a guy with kids?" Abby asked.

Squinting, Heather pondered. "I'd bone him, for sure. Jeremy's hot in a geeky author sort of way. He'd probably correct my grammar as I blew him off."

Justine broke into laughter at the hilarious mental image.

"But if he wanted me to interact with his spawns, I'd be out. Kids are like weird little aliens to me, and I have no idea what to do around them. So, there's the potential for something physical with him if he's into it, but that's all I've got on that front."

"Well, Gary took to my kid like a fish to water, so never say never," Justine said, arching a brow.

"Gary's a good one. I really like him, Justine."

"He sure is."

"Have you guys said the 'L' word yet? Chad said it to me first, which I'll never let him live down."

Justine chewed as she contemplated. "We haven't, which is kind of strange because we've discussed a lot of serious stuff like marriage and having a kid together. I think we both were holding back because we didn't want the other to think we were moving too fast. That's kind of silly at this point though. I should really tell him."

"So, this is it?" Abby asked, excitement flaring in her eyes. "We're going to have another wedding in Ardor Creek?"

"I think so. We just need to figure out the logistics."

"Well, here's to wedded bliss and all," Heather said, lifting her glass. "Hope it goes better for you this time, Jus."

"Me too," she said, laughing as they clinked their glasses. "Actually, scratch that. I have no doubt. Gary and I are going to crush marriage this time around."

"Hear, hear," the ladies chimed, thrilled for their friend and thankful for the foundation of new friendships forged in their tiny town.

Chapter 22

G ary spent weeks alternating his busy work schedule and planning his surprise proposal for Justine. As January turned to February, the stress of his busy life began to chip away at his usually calm and steady attitude. Justine had stopped taking the pill, telling him she wanted to give her body ample time to adjust. That was fine since they'd discussed it at length, but it created extra pressure in the bedroom, which messed with his mind. He found himself barely able to perform and collapsed on the bed, frustrated, one night as they tried to make love.

"Hey," Justine said, rolling over and sliding her leg over his thighs as he lay on his back atop the crisp sheets. "It's okay, Gary. We've had a long day, and we're exhausted."

"It's not okay, Jus. I don't want to tie you to someone who can't give you what you want."

"All I want is you," she said, kissing his chin. "If we can't get pregnant this way, there are other methods."

"All of which require you enduring procedures that are risky and cost tons of money. I'm not sure it's worth it for you, Jus."

When she didn't respond, he lifted his gaze to find tears glistening in her eyes. Feeling like an ass, he cupped her cheek. "I'm sorry. Please don't cry. I'm terrible at this. I just want to give you what you deserve, honey."

"Here's the thing," she said, gently running her palm over his chest. "You give me everything, Gary. You love my little girl to distraction, and you treat me like a queen. But I'm not going to let you sabotage our relationship with old fears from your last one. We both deserve better than that."

"We do," he whispered, wondering if he was going to lose her.

"So, here's what we're going to do." Sitting up, she slowly climbed from the bed and began to tug on her clothes. "I'm going to go home and leave you here to think about what you really want."

Sitting up in bed, he rested his arms over his knees as his heart slowly broke into a thousand pieces. Once she was dressed, she sat on the edge of the bed and gave him a slow kiss. "I was excited to hang here with you tonight since my parents are watching Avery, but I'm not entering into a future where you focus on your performance issues. They're real and they suck, but they certainly don't define our relationship."

"I know they don't—"

"For you, they still do," she interjected, covering his lips with her fingers. "And you're going to have to find a way to let go of that. Maybe you should talk to Teresa. She's really awesome, and I know she wouldn't make you feel embarrassed in any way."

Inhaling a deep breath, he nodded. "I can try."

Standing, she smiled at him, her eyes filled with such compassion and love. "Your sexual performance has zero effect on how much I love you, Gary. Zilch." Holding up her hand, she formed a circle with her fingers and thumb. "Nada. But I can't console you each time it happens and you can't freak out either. We have to just acknowledge it and move on. Hell, maybe we can even laugh about it one day. But that's up to you."

"Jus..." he whispered.

"Don't say it back," she said, holding up her hand. "I know it's true, but I don't want the words from you when you're frustrated and when I'm about to walk out the door. I want them from you when you're ready to accept that I love you enough to accept every part of you." Leaning in, she pressed a kiss to his lips. "Good night. Figure it out soon because I don't want to sleep without you." With one last heartbreaking smile, she left him and trailed through the door.

Groaning in frustration, he fell back on the bed and ran his fingers through his hair. Picking up his phone from the nightstand, he dialed Mark.

"Hey, man. Thought you were with Jus."

"I was, but we...well, we didn't fight, necessarily, but she wanted to give me space to think about some stuff."

Silence stretched through the phone. "Did you fuck it up, Gary? Tell me you didn't fuck it up."

"I'm trying not to. I need to talk to Teresa. Is she there?"

"Sure. One sec." Something shuffled in the background before Teresa said, "Gary? It's nice to hear from you. How are you?"

"Not great, Teresa. I think I need to schedule a session with you or whatever. The sooner the better."

"No problem. We could just meet at one of our houses if that works for you."

"I'm off tomorrow. I can Venmo you for the session if you take that form of payment."

"Don't be silly. I don't charge friends, Gary. Hold on a minute." He heard her muffled conversation with Mark before she spoke. "I can be at your house at 10:00 a.m."

"Perfect. I assume Jus already told you about my issues. I don't mind that she did. I know you all are close. I mean, it's not something I want shared with the world, but I know you wouldn't say anything."

"I haven't even told Mark," she said before Mark yelled in the background, "*Told me what?*"

"Nothing, dear," she chimed, emitting a small chuckle. "We can discuss anything you like, Gary. See you tomorrow."

"Thanks, Teresa. I really appreciate it. I know your life is as busy as mine."

"I always have time for my friends. Good night."

Hanging up the phone, Gary settled into bed for a long night of tossing and turning, knowing the anxiety of losing Justine would keep him awake long into the night.

T he next morning, Gary prepared a large pot of coffee so he and Teresa could drink it while they spoke. She arrived at his door looking fresh and rested, which was the polar opposite of how he felt. He'd barely slept at all while wondering if he'd fucked everything up for good. Teresa stepped inside, and he led her to the living room before offering her a cup of coffee.

"Only cream, please," she said, sitting on the couch.

"Be right back."

Returning with two full cups, he sat on the other end of the sofa and asked about Rose before Teresa gently smiled. "I absolutely love talking about my daughter, but I think we're here to discuss you."

Sighing, he rubbed his forehead. "I'm a mess from this, Teresa. Justine left last night, and she had every right to. She swears she doesn't care about my performance issues, but how is that possible? She wants to have another child, and I feel so selfish for tying her to someone like me who might not be able to give her one."

"From what I've observed of your treatment of Justine and Avery, you are the opposite of selfish, but I understand your fears. Why don't you tell me exactly what happened last night? After that, I'd like to hear a bit about how things went when you didn't sexually perform with your ex-wife. It's possible you're having trouble mentally separating the reactions of both partners, and I can work with that, but I need the full story."

Nodding, he stared into his black coffee. "This is really hard to talk about."

"I know," she said with a gentle nod. "Nothing you say to me will leave this room."

Inhaling a deep breath, he began to divulge everything to her. Nicole's reactions in the past, Justine's extreme patience since they began dating, and the surfacing of his frustration the previous evening.

"Okay," she said after he'd bared his soul. "I think I see what's going on. Justine going off the pill added an extra layer of pressure that you didn't really prepare yourself for. It was easier for you to believe she didn't care about your issues when there was nothing at stake."

"And now, everything is at stake. I can't promise her I can give her what she wants. It's heartbreaking, and she deserves better."

"Justine deserves exactly what she asks of you. Has she been open to other methods if you can't conceive naturally?"

"She says she is."

Setting aside her empty coffee cup, she smiled. "Then you have to believe her. What you're really experiencing is a trust issue, not a sexual one. You're not trusting her, and that's very hurtful to a partner. I can see why she left. It must be devastating to feel a certain way and have your partner completely discount that feeling."

"Shit," he muttered, rubbing his forehead. "I don't want to discount her feelings."

"But you're doing it every time she reassures you it's not an issue and you dismiss her. A self-respecting woman will only put up with that for so long."

"Nicole said it wasn't an issue in the beginning, but it wasn't true. How do I know Justine won't change her mind?"

Teresa's lips curved into a brilliant smile. "Unless you're a fortune-teller, you can't. Relationships are hard, Gary. You know that from your divorce. But your relationship certainly won't succeed if you keep dismissing Justine's feelings. Nicole was a different woman and is a part of your past. You have the opportunity to write a new future with a woman who loves you and accepts every part of you. I know it's scary, but so is anything that matters."

"*She* matters," Gary said, rubbing his hand over his heart. "She's all that's mattered to me for so long. I think I convinced myself I didn't deserve her."

"All that matters is whether *she* thinks you deserve her." Leaning forward, she winked. "And let me tell you, she gushes over you, Gary. She's enamored with how you treat her and Avery. Don't let your fears destroy your happiness. Life is too damn short."

"Your husband gave me the same advice."

Chuckling, she lifted a shoulder. "Well, we almost fucked it up ourselves, so we're good examples. Thankfully, we were able to overcome our fears and finally be honest with each other. Are you able to do the same? Your situation is a bit different. You need to overcome your fear of accepting yourself exactly how you are and believing Justine could accept you that way too."

"And if she comes to resent me one day?" he asked softly.

"Then at least you tried. Wouldn't you rather look back and know you tried instead of pushing her toward someone else? Could you really live with that?"

"No," he whispered, shaking his head.

"Then get your crap together and go tell her you love her, you big idiot."

Laughing, he squinted one eye. "Is that official advice, Dr. Lancaster-Roe?"

"You're damn straight it is."

Rising, they hugged each other before drawing back. "If I figure this out, I aim to make us official in-laws, Teresa. I was already planning something huge before I fucked up. Want to hear about it? I'm dying to tell someone."

"Oh, do tell," she said, waggling her eyebrows.

Brimming with excitement, Gary told her as she listened with delight. Then, he threw on his boots and headed over to Justine's house to fix what he'd broken.

Chapter 23

Justine sat at the kitchen island drinking a glass of wine as she scrolled through Instagram. Avery was at the movies with Mark, Peter, and his kids, and the silence reminded her of the loneliness she'd felt before Gary. She didn't usually have wine at eleven o'clock on a Sunday, but she felt awful about how things had gone last night and figured wine couldn't make it any worse.

Sighing, she replayed the events in her head for the hundredth time, wondering if she'd done the right thing by leaving. She truly believed it was imperative they addressed Gary's frustration now before they continued down the road of getting married and trying to conceive a child. It had broken her heart to leave him, but she felt they needed a tiny break to evaluate how to move forward. Now, half a day later, she second-guessed herself. Teresa had encouraged her to be supportive and she'd still left him, as Nicole had emotionally left him in their marriage. Tiny bugs of anxiety buzzed in her stomach as she debated what to do next.

Hearing a rustling at the front door, her head snapped, and she lurched to her feet. Grabbing a knife from the block, she held it high, ready to plunge it into Dean's throat if he dared step into her house.

"Justine?" Gary called, walking into the kitchen. Staring at her with wide eyes, he held up his hands. "Jesus, woman. I know we fought, but was it that bad?"

Relief swamped her as she closed her eyes. Placing her hand over her heart, she began to laugh. "I thought you were Dean. Holy shit."

"Sorry, honey," he said, tentatively approaching. Encircling her hand, he withdrew the knife and set it on the island. "I'd like to talk without weapons if possible."

Overcome with laughter, she bounded into his arms, squeezing him tight as she buried her face in his neck. "I'm so sorry," she said, kissing the pulsing vein above the neckline of his sweater.

"I*m* sorry," he said, kissing her hair as his hands roved over her back. "I really fucked up, Jus."

Drawing back, she gazed into his eyes. "You didn't. I just felt like we weren't communicating, and I didn't know how to handle it."

"You were communicating just fine," he said, cupping her cheeks. "I was the ass who wasn't listening."

"I meaaaaan, if you want to take the blame, I'll let you, although it takes two to tango, buddy."

Chuckling, he swooped in for a kiss. "That it does. I called Teresa and she came over this morning."

"Oh, that's awesome. She's so good at this stuff."

"She is," he said with a nod. "I'm going to keep seeing her every two weeks until I feel like I don't need to. I think it will help me as we build our life together, Jus."

"Our life together," she said wistfully. "I like the sound of that."

Sliding his arm around her waist, he pulled her close, aligning their bodies as he reverently gazed into her eyes. Love swam in his gorgeous brown orbs, and she was overcome with the realization she'd finally found her soul mate.

"Justine Lancaster, I've loved you for so long. So. Damn. Long. I was in love with you all those years ago after my divorce, when I used to show up at your house and check on you and Avery."

His features blurred as tears welled in her eyes. "I had no idea because I thought I was in love with a man who isn't anything close to the man you are, Gary. God, I could kick myself."

His thumbs stroked her cheeks as he continued. "I loved you the night of your arrest, and my heart broke at what you endured. Seeing your strength that night only made me love you more."

Scoffing, she gave him a playful glare. "I was a hot mess that night, but whatever."

"That was the first night I used handcuffs on you," he said, waggling his brows.

Tossing back her head, she broke into a joyful laugh. "But not the last, buddy."

"Not by a long shot." Resting his forehead on hers, he stared deeply into her eyes. "I love you so much more every single day, which I didn't realize was possible before you. I'm sorry I didn't tell you sooner. I was scared I wasn't enough for you. That you deserved better."

Tears skated down her cheeks as she tried to form a response to his heart-wrenching words. "Gary," she whispered, shaking her head against his. "I love you more each day too. I need you to believe me because nothing has ever been more real to me."

"I do believe you, Jus, and I'm going to work on recognizing my fears for what they are when they surface. I want to laugh with you when we make love. I want it to be something you enjoy."

"I do," she said, sliding her fingers in his hair. "I love everything we do together. Whether it's you holding me or kissing me or being inside me. If we can't make a baby the natural way, at least we'll die trying."

Laughter burst from his throat. "What a way to go."

Encircling his wrists, she glided his hands down her body and molded his palms to her ass. "Now that we've established that we freaking love each other, I'd really like you to take me upstairs and fuck me, Officer Lincoln."

Emitting that sexy growl that melted her panties, he crouched down and lifted her. Justine wrapped her legs around his waist, clutching his shoulders as he carried her up the stairs.

"God, I love it when you carry me," she murmured, kissing his neck as he crossed the threshold to her bedroom.

He tossed her on the bed and reached for the button of her jeans before she swatted him away. "I'll get them. Take yours off."

They fumbled with their clothes, practically ripping them off, until they were both naked. Gary grabbed her ankles and pulled her to the edge of the bed. Dropping to his knees, he gripped her inner thighs and pushed them apart before burying his face in her dripping pussy.

"*Oh, god,*" she cried, head tossed back on the comforter as his lips devoured her quivering flesh. "Yesssss...you're really going for it...*ohhhhh....*"

His soft chuckle reverberated over her wet folds as she relaxed against his mouth. He swiped that talented tongue up and down her slit, adding to the wetness as he consumed her. "Wrap your legs around my head and pull me into you."

"You're going to suffocate."

"I don't give a damn. Do it, Jus. I need my hands."

Listening to her man, she wrapped her legs around his head, pulling him into her core. Gary spread her wide, licking her one last, thorough time before placing his lips over her opening. Holding her apart, he thrust his tongue into her wet channel, impaling her before retracting and surging forth again. Gliding two fingers to her clit, he stimulated the sensitive spot as he fucked her with his tongue. Justine moaned, overcome with the quick gyrations of his fingers on her tight nub as his tongue entered and retreated.

"So fucking good..." she wailed, sliding her hands to her breasts and pinching her nipples, adding to the sensation. "Oh, god...right there..."

Gary groaned into her mound, his motions frenzied as he worked her body toward its peak. Her muscles began to tremble, and she clutched the comforter in tight fists, needing a stronghold as he took her higher. His grunts and growls were so damn sexy against her wet flesh, and she felt the orgasm looming on the horizon.

Screaming his name, her back arched, pushing her further into his skillful mouth. Feeling her spine snap, she wailed with pleasure as the orgasm claimed her. Stars burst behind her closed eyelids, and she laughed with joy between her satiated groans. Gary murmured words of love against her deepest place, and she reveled in how selfless he was to always ensure her pleasure first.

Squeezing his head with her thighs, she silently told him to stop. Her body was now a quaking mess of frayed nerves, and she trembled upon the bed as he lifted his head.

"That really turned me on, if you get my drift," he said, excitement in his gaze.

"Fuck me," she commanded, understanding he was aroused. "The lube is in the drawer."

Reaching over, he opened the drawer and found the container, opening it and setting it on the nightstand. He gathered the glistening substance on his fingers before sliding them over his hard cock. Gazing into her eyes, he stroked long and slow as he maneuvered between her legs. Aligning the blunt head of his shaft with her opening, he gazed into her eyes as he began to push inside.

"Mine," he growled, grabbing her ankles and lifting them high.

"All yours," she sighed, opening to him as he thrust into her core. He began to slide back and forth, and Justine could read the pleasure in his eyes that he was able to love her this way.

Lowering her legs, he slithered over her and glided a hand behind her knee. Lifting her leg high, he surged inside as he stared deep into her eyes.

"Justine," he whispered, sweat covering his brow as he worked his body against hers. "For so damn long, I only wanted to be right here."

"You made it," she teased, cupping his jaw. "And you're doing a very good job, Officer Lincoln."

Breathing a laugh, he increased the pace of his hips. Licking his fingers, he dropped them to her clit, circling as her eyes lit with pleasure. Their bodies worked in tandem as they loved each other, and she was overcome by their connection.

"I love you," she whispered, sliding her fingers into his thick hair. "So much, Gary."

"I love you, Jus," he rasped, jutting his cock deep into her wet core. "You're everything."

She speared her nails into his scalp, causing him to groan. "I'm going to come again," she whimpered, her climax close from the ministrations of his fingers on her clit.

"Come with me, honey," he gritted, closing his eyes as he dragged his shaft through her drenched channel. "I'm so close."

Wrapping her legs around his back, she held on for dear life as the orgasm claimed her. Gary moaned as her inner muscles began to spasm around his cock. Burying his face in her neck, he began to come, spurting jets of release inside her core as her tight walls milked him.

"*Fuck!*" he cried into her sweat-soaked neck, causing Justine to break into gleeful laughter. Their bodies quaked and shuddered against each other until he relaxed on top of her, sated and replete. Expelling a large breath, he sighed her name.

Justine stroked his scalp in soft, sure strokes until he slowly lifted his head and gave her a huge smile. Lifting a weak arm, she held up her palm. Snickering, Gary gave her a high-five before collapsing against her again.

"I told you we were going to reach simultaneous orgasm and give each other a high-five," she said, giggling. "We did it. I'm proud of us."

Gary encircled her with his arms, snuggling with her as their bodies cooled. "We're sex rock stars."

Their chuckles mingled as they softly caressed each other, and Justine's eyes began to droop. "Thirty-minute naked power nap before Avery gets home? We can do it."

"I'm already half-asleep. Wake me up in thirty minutes."

"*You* have to wake *me* up," she chided.

"Mm-hmm..."

His soft snores were the last sounds she heard as she slipped into her dreams.

Chapter 24

Gary awoke on Valentine's Day ready to implement his plan. After everything was set with Heather later that afternoon, he lifted his phone from his pocket and called Carrie.

"Hey, hey!" she said, her tone excited. "We're all set here at the pub."

"Thanks so much for helping me with this, Carrie."

"Are you kidding? It's so romantic. Go get 'em, Officer."

Chuckling, he grinned at his reflection in the mirror attached to the foyer wall. "On my way. See you soon."

Gathering his keys and the other essentials he needed for the evening, he stepped out the front door and locked it behind him. The drive to Justine's was short, and he parked in their driveway as Avery jogged through the front door.

"Do you like my dress, Gary?" she asked, holding open her coat so Gary could see her pretty pink dress. "Mom said I could wear it since I'm going on the Valentine's date with you."

"You look like a pretty princess," he said, crouching so he was on eye level with her. "And you've got all these sparkly things in your hair."

"They're sparkle clips," she said, touching the accessories that lined her golden hair.

"Like mother, like daughter," Justine said, appearing beside her. "She wanted different colored sparkle clips, so that's where we're at."

Laughing, he stood and kissed her before drawing back and giving a low whistle. "You look beautiful, Jus."

"Oh, this old thing?" she asked, running a hand over her red dress as she held open her black coat. "It's not like I spent all week looking for the perfect dress or anything. I haven't been out on a proper Valentine's date in forever."

"Well, let's get this show on the road. I've got two beautiful ladies to attend to."

Avery giggled as he opened the back door. Once she was situated and Justine was in the front seat, Gary slid behind the wheel and began the drive toward Main Street.

"You're a real trooper to let her tag along tonight," Justine said, sliding her hand over his and threading their fingers. "I swear, every babysitter I called was busy tonight. I know it's Saturday and Valentine's Day, but I figured *someone* would be available."

Gary grinned, secretly aware that he'd spread the word to all the babysitters in Ardor Creek to tell Justine they weren't available. He needed both his girls present for what he had planned.

"Uh, I thought we were going to dinner at the Italian place," she said as he drove through Main Street and didn't stop to park at the restaurant.

"We are," he said, kissing her hand. "But I have a stop to make first."

"Okaaaaay," she said, narrowing her eyes. "I'm not sure that's a good idea with a hungry kid in tow, but let's try it."

"Believe me, it will be worth it."

He drove onto Cyprus Street and parked in the driveway of the house for sale on the edge of the cul-de-sac. Turning off the car, he stepped out and opened Avery's door, helping her out before jogging around and urging Justine from the car.

"Are we getting a tour of the house? I wasn't sure you liked it."

"Let's check it out and see. Come on." Turning to Avery, he picked her up and situated her on his hip before taking Justine's hand. They walked to the front door, and Gary pulled the key Heather had given him from his pocket. Unlocking the door, he urged them inside.

"I love the living room," Justine said, slowly perusing the room as Gary closed the front door and set Avery on her feet. "It's so spacious."

"I think you'll like the upstairs den even better," he said, pointing to the stairs. "The heat's on, so we can take off our coats." He shrugged his off before taking Justine and Avery's coats and laying them over the stair rail. Extending his hand, he smiled when Justine tentatively took it. Avery began walking up the stairs, and he tugged Justine's hand.

"What the heck is going on, Gary? You're acting weird."

He led her up the stairs to the den, where he'd set up a circular table lined with red rose petals. A bottle of champagne was chilling alongside a bottle of apple juice. Several red and pink helium balloons hung against the ceiling, and Avery gasped.

"Balloons!"

"Here you go," Gary said, pulling one down and handing her the string. "Now, let's get you ladies situated. Avery, you're going to stand here." He gently maneuvered her beside the table with the champagne. "And Justine," he said, leading her over, "you're going to stand here."

His girls looked at him as if he were slightly insane as he stood before them in his dress shirt and slacks. Reaching under the red tablecloth, he pulled out a sport coat, shrugging it on before patting it flat. "I need to look presentable for this. What do you think, Ave?"

"You look nice," she said with a nod.

"Thank you."

Reaching into his pocket, he pulled out two felt-covered boxes, one pink and one black, and set them on the table. "I have a present for each of you, but I'm going to start with Avery."

Justine's lips pursed before she covered them with her fingers. "Gary…" she warbled.

"Don't cry, honey," he teased, picking up the pink box. "I haven't done anything yet."

She laughed as Gary lowered to one knee in front of Avery. Opening the pink box, he showed her the gold necklace inside with a heart-shaped pendant. "Avery Lancaster, you are the most special little girl I've ever met, and I love you very much."

"I love you too, Gary," she said, giving him a shy smile.

"I got you this necklace as a reminder of the promise I want to make you and your mom." Removing the necklace, he fastened it around her neck, drawing the pendant to lay over her chest. "This heart is a symbol of how much I love you." He tapped the gold heart. "I want to ask your mom to marry me, but only if you say yes first."

"You can marry Mom!" she said excitedly. "And we can be a family."

Feeling his eyes well, he cleared his throat. "That means a whole lot, Avery." Drawing her into his arms, he squeezed as her small arms hugged him back. "I love you, sweetheart."

"Love you," she said softly.

Drawing back, he smoothed a hand over her hair before rising to observe the tears streaming down Justine's face. Reaching into his pocket, he handed her a fresh tissue. Laughing, she took it and wiped away the tears before blowing her nose.

"Gross," she said, rolling her eyes. "I'm trying not to scare you away before you propose." She stuffed the tissue in her tiny purse before setting it on the table.

"I think you're going to be fine," he teased, reaching for the black box. Lowering to one knee, he flipped open the ring box and stared into her stunning eyes. "Justine Lancaster—"

"Yes!" she cried as Avery snickered below.

"One dang minute, woman," he said, playfully rolling his eyes. Clearing his throat, he continued. "Justine, I'm not eloquent enough to make a rousing speech about how amazing and special you are. I wish I was, but we've all got our limitations. What I will say is that I didn't even understand what true love was until I fell bone-deep into it with you. You and Avery are my entire world, and I want to spend the rest of my life loving you both with my whole heart. Will you make me the luckiest man in the world and marry me already?"

Tossing back her head, she broke into joyful laughter. "Already? I thought you'd never ask. Yes, you daft man. Put the ring on my finger!"

Their laughter mingled as he slipped the princess-cut diamond ring onto her finger. Rising, Gary pulled her into his arms for a torrid kiss as Avery covered her mouth and giggled below.

"And what are you laughing at, young lady?" Gary asked, ending the kiss and winking at Avery.

"You guys are kissing and it's gross. But you can marry Mom anyway."

"Well, thank you." Pressing one last kiss to Justine's lips, Gary turned toward the table and arranged three plastic champagne flutes. Opening the bottles of champagne and apple juice, he poured them and handed them to his girls.

"To our new family," he said before they clinked the glasses together. "And to what I hope will be our new house."

They sipped as Justine's eyes darted around the den. "How did you set this up?"

"Heather helped me. You're right, she's pretty cool. I want to buy it, Jus, as long as you still want to buy it with me. I figured it's never too early to start making memories in a new home, right?"

"Right," she said, sliding her arm around his waist. "I love this freaking house. Let's do it."

"I get the biggest room," Avery said, raising her hand.

"Whoever gets the biggest room has to do the most chores," Justine said, arching a brow.

Avery's lips formed a frown. "Okay, maybe the *second* biggest room."

"We'll see."

"And I want a dog, Mommy," she whined.

Justine shot Gary an acerbic glare. "Always with the 'Mommy' when she wants something. Get ready. You're going to be 'Daddy' soon. It's hard to say no."

Breathing a laugh, he nodded. "Noted."

"Please, please, please?" Avery said, jumping up and down.

"Let's not spill apple juice over the carpet before we buy it, sweetie," she said. "But we'll consider a dog. I think it would be nice and teach you responsibility."

"Thank you, Mom." She flashed a beaming smile.

Eventually, they walked through the house, Avery detailing where every piece of furniture would go as the adults chuckled. Once they'd seen the house, Gary informed them he planned to come back and clean up tomorrow.

"For now, I want to take you out to celebrate. Come on, ladies."

They hopped back in the car, and Gary drove them to Main Street. Parking in front of the pub, he urged them to follow him inside.

"Let's tell Terry we're engaged," he said to Justine as they walked across the sidewalk. "She'll get a kick out of it."

"Sure," Justine said with a shrug.

Gary pulled open the pub door, and they walked inside to the rousing scream of, "Surprise!"

Justine's mouth fell open as she gaped at Gary. "What is this?"

"It's a surprise engagement party," he said, gesturing to all of their friends who lined the main room of the pub. "You already knew everyone in Ardor Creek was going to be up in our business. I figured, why not make a party out of it?" Glancing over at Terry behind the bar, Gary lifted his hand to his mouth and yelled, "Hit it, Terry!"

"I got you, Gary!" she yelled back. Her fingers darted over the black remote that controlled the jukebox before "Holiday" by Madonna began to blare from the speakers. "Come on, ladies," he said, taking Justine and Avery's hands. "Let's dance."

He led them to the dance floor, where they were promptly joined by Mark, Teresa, Ashlyn, Scott, Carrie, Peter, Abby, Chad, and the rest of the Ardor Creek crew. Adults and kids all danced to the rhythm of the catchy song as love and excitement swam in Justine's eyes.

"Wow!" she yelled over the music. "This is way better than getting proposed to at McDonald's!"

Laughter bounded from his throat as he pulled her close. "I wanted it to be special. I love you so much, Jus."

"I love you," she said, palming his cheeks and smacking a kiss on his lips. "Let's show marriage how awesome we can be. The first time was a practice round. We're going to rock it this time."

"We're going to kick marriage's ass," he affirmed with a nod.

Overcome with laughter, they tugged Avery close, cementing their family bond as their friends surrounded them in the beloved watering hole of Ardor Creek.

Epilogue

♥

Two days before Christmas

G ary stood over Justine's shoulder in the hotel bathroom as she held the pregnancy test in her hands. Staring up at him, she grinned before playfully shoving him away. "Get out of here. I just peed on the damn thing. It takes a few minutes, Gary."

"I know," he said, his lips forming a cute frown as he cupped her shoulder. "But you were such a trooper when you did the IUI procedure, and I don't want you to have to go through that again. I hope this one worked and we can just relax and be pregnant."

"Um, there's nothing relaxing about being pregnant, but whatever you say," she teased. Finding his gaze in the mirror, she leaned back against his bare chest. "And the procedure was no big deal. You married a tough broad."

"Don't I know it," he said, kissing her light purple hair. She'd dyed it recently, knowing it might be the last time she could before getting pregnant.

"Did you speak to your parents?" she asked, concern in her gaze. "They've been so great during this whole Florida trip, but an entire day with Avery at Epcot Center might be too much."

"They texted twenty minutes ago that they're having a grand ol' time," he said, nipping her shoulder. "And as much I've enjoyed the trip, I needed a few hours alone with you, hon."

Smiling, she glanced at the pregnancy test again, wondering how long it was going to take for the symbols to appear. "A week is definitely long enough. After staying two days at their house and three days here at the resort, I'm ready to get back to Ardor Creek the day after Christmas. Does that make me a small-town hick?"

Laughing, he shrugged. "If you're one, so am I. I love our town."

"Me too." Squinting, she saw the blue lines begin to materialize on the stick. Sucking in a breath, she watched as the plus sign appeared above the straight line.

"Holy shit," she whispered, glancing up at Gary.

"Plus means pregnant," he said with awe as his eyes widened. "I memorized it so I didn't forget."

"Plus means pregnant," she affirmed. Setting the test on the bathroom counter, she faced him and slid her arms around his neck. "Officer Lincoln, you have been a *very* bad boy and knocked up your wife. What am I going to do with you?"

Elation contorted his features as he hugged her so tight she struggled to breathe. "I can't believe it worked. Holy shit, Jus! It worked."

Pulling back, she nodded as she stared into his eyes. "It worked. I hope you're ready for this."

"I'm so freaking ready," he said, resting his forehead against hers. Sliding his hands to her ass, he cupped the tender flesh under her thin shorts and squeezed. "Let's celebrate."

Emitting a sultry chuckle, she pressed her body against his. "What did you have in mind?"

Lifting her by the globes of her ass, he carried her to the large bed and gently placed her on the white sheets. Gliding over her, he nudged her nose with his. "I figured we could start with me kissing you about a million times."

Sighing, she threaded her fingers through his hair. "Officer Lincoln, I sure do love the way you celebrate." Giving him a sweet kiss, she gently urged his head lower. "Go on and give it a try. We have three hours until your parents return with Child Number One."

His sexy laugh surrounded her as his lips began to trail kisses over her neck and the smooth skin between her breasts. Justine lost count somewhere between one and a million, but whatever the final number was, her husband certainly excelled at celebratory kisses.

Before You Go

Well, awesome readers, you asked for Justine and Gary's story, and I heard you loud and clear! Hope you enjoyed their sweet, steamy story as much as I did. And by now, you know I've already set up another Ardor Creek couple in my head, right? I think our sexy, geeky author Jeremy needs to have some fun with former bad girl Heather. She's been burned and swears she only wants some sexy shenanigans, but I'm convinced Ardor Creek's newest resident can help her believe in love again. You can read Heather and Jeremy's story in **Futures Entwined**. Enjoy!

Please consider leaving a review on your retailer's site, Book-Bub, and/or Goodreads. Your reviews help spread the word for indie authors so we can keep writing smokin' hot books for you to devour. Thanks so much for reading!

About the Author

♥

Ayla Asher is the pen name for a USA Today bestselling author who writes steamy fantasy romance under a different pseudonym. However, she loves a spicy, fast-paced contemporary romance too! Therefore, she's decided to share some of her contemporary stories, hoping to spread a little joy one HEA at a time. She would love to connect with you on social media, where she enjoys making dorky TikToks, FB/IG posts and fun book trailers!

ALSO BY AYLA ASHER

Manhattan Holiday Loves Trilogy
Book 1: His Holiday Pact
Book 2: Her Valentine Surprise
Book 3: Her Patriotic Prince

Ardor Creek Series
Book 1: Hearts Reclaimed
Book 2: Illusions Unveiled
Book 3: Desires Uncovered
Book 4: Resolutions Embraced
Book 5: Passions Fulfilled
Book 6: Futures Entwined